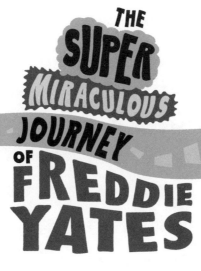

THE
SUPER
MIRACULOUS
JOURNEY
OF FREDDIE
YATES

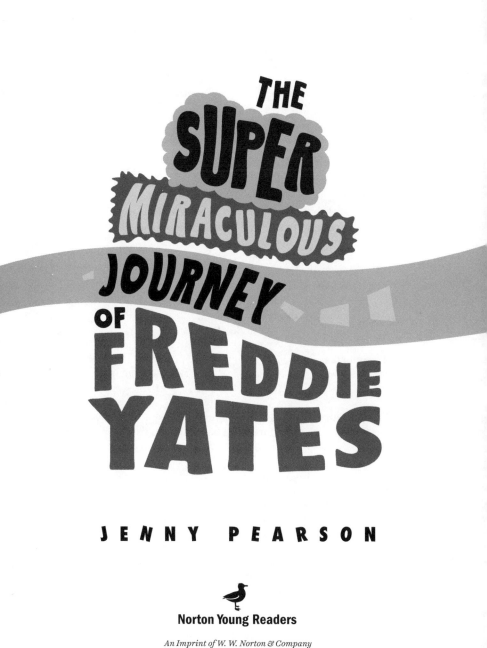

THE SUPER MIRACULOUS JOURNEY OF FREDDIE YATES

JENNY PEARSON

Norton Young Readers

An Imprint of W. W. Norton & Company
Independent Publishers Since 1923

For information about permission to reproduce selections
from this book, write to Permissions, W. W. Norton & Company, Inc.,
500 Fifth Avenue, New York, NY 10110

For information about special discounts for bulk purchases, please
contact W. W. Norton Special Sales at specialsales@wwnorton.com
or 800-233-4830

Manufacturing by Sheridan
Book design by Chris Welch
Production manager: Anna Oler

ISBN 978-1-324-01133-0

W. W. Norton & Company, Inc.
500 Fifth Avenue, New York, N.Y. 10110
www.wwnorton.com

W. W. Norton & Company Ltd.
15 Carlisle Street, London W1D 3BS

1 2 3 4 5 6 7 8 9 0

For William and Douglas, my miracles.
And to Andrew who helped make them.

Miracles might come in all shapes and sizes, but I'm still not convinced they are small and furry like Lady Gaga

It's funny what people consider to be a miracle. After Dad had his "little accident," Grams said, "Joe, it's a small miracle you didn't kill yourself." It wasn't a small miracle, though, it was Eileen from the hairdresser's and nothing about Eileen is small or miraculous. If she hadn't been walking her dog, Lady Gaga, at that exact moment, she wouldn't have seen Dad's mail truck roll down the hill and shouted at him to move out of the way. So, as I said—not a miracle, just good timing. Well good-ish timing—he still broke his leg.

Our teacher, Mrs. Walker, once said that if she finished the school year without strangling one of us it would be a miracle. At the end of sixth year, all my class were still alive . . . at least I *think* they were still alive. Dylan Katano disappeared midway through the fall term, but

I heard he went back to Japan. Anyway, my point is that Mrs. Walker was wrong. Not strangling one of 6W is not a miracle—even if we were a handful.

In the olden days miracles used to be bigger. Although there's no knowing if those miracles actually happened. Once Charlie, Ben, and I tried to share a bag of fish and chips from Marley's. It stretched the very limits of our friendship—and Marley's is known for their big portions. How some guy called Jesus managed to share three haddock and some white bread with 5,000 people, I do not know. I guess people *wanted* to believe it had happened.

Dad says people like a good story, and if it makes them happy then why let the truth get in the way? I suppose that's what happened in Wales this summer. People saw what they wanted to see. And they wanted to see miracles.

If you'd have asked me at the beginning of July what I thought about that, I'd have told you that the truth is important. That facts are important. Back then, facts were just about my favorite thing. Some people collect Pokémon cards, some people collect stickers, I collected facts. See, once you know a fact, it's yours to keep forever. It can't leave you and no one can take it away. But then, this summer I saw something truly miraculous that made me question everything.

1

You probably need to know a bit about Ben and Charlie to understand why they got involved in this whole thing

The summer should have gone like this—Ben was supposed to be going to America with his dad and his new stepmom Becky, Charlie was going to some vegan sanctuary with his parents, and I was going to be hanging around the house with Dad and Grams. But none of this happened.

On the surface you might think Ben had the best deal. But you haven't met Becky. Even Disney World can't cancel out Becky. Grams said she'd met women like her before. I don't know who these women were or where she met them, but I got the impression Grams did not approve.

On the last day of sixth year we sang a really shouty version of "One More Step Along the World I Go" in our final assembly. Then Mrs. Walker wished us and our future teachers the best of luck and led us out to the playground to be picked up by our parents. She looked pretty frazzled by then. Ben had put a packet of Mentos in a bottle of Coke at the class party and there had been a massive explosion. He said he didn't know it would happen, but we all knew that was a lie because a lively woman with striped tights and a badge that said *I Love Science* had done it in assembly in fifth year.

I had permission to walk home as Dad couldn't drive after his accident and Grams wasn't allowed to drive after she crashed into the war memorial in the center of town. I think the doctor said it was because she had guacamole in her eyes—which is odd because she didn't like Mexican food. (She also couldn't have driven me home because by this point she was dead—but I didn't know that at the time. I'm telling you now so you're prepared for the sad part later.)

Ben, Charlie, and I were walking out of the school gates—I was heading to the newsstand to buy my usual after-school snack of a bag of Monster Munch—when Ben's new stepmom Becky rolled up in their new Range Rover and wound down the window. She was wearing a very low-cut top that Grams would have said is "just asking for attention."

"Hi, boys!" She smiled, revealing a *lot* of teeth. Actually, I have a fact about teeth—you might want to write this down, it's a good one. Grown-up humans have thirty-two teeth. Which, in the animal kingdom, is not that many. Most people think sharks have the most teeth, but they're wrong. The garden snail has over 14,000 teeth. Even Becky doesn't have that many.

Charlie whistled and said something embarrassing like, "Your new mom is awesome!"

Ben didn't like that, so he gave Charlie a shove—not hard though. Ben reckons Charlie doesn't have a filter. He'll just blurt out whatever he's thinking. I reckon Ben's right about that.

Anyway, Becky flicked her long blonde hair and lifted up her huge sunglasses. "Hop in, Ben, I'm taking you for a haircut before our family vacation. You're looking shabby."

Ben wasn't looking shabby. He has this really cool flattop going on. Sometimes he even has zigzag lines or patterns shaved into the sides. The girls seem to like it. Well, they like it more than the haircut Grams gave me with the pinking shears that left me with crinkly bangs. She blamed that on the guacamole too.

Ben was definitely upset by the "shabby" comment. He takes his hair quite seriously. He stuffed his hands in his pockets and mumbled so Becky couldn't hear but I heard what he said. He said, "She's not my *new mom*. She's not even family."

Becky didn't like being kept waiting. Her face got a bit ugly and she shouted, "Benjamin!"

He seemed to get smaller and muttered, "It's *Ben*."

Everyone knows he doesn't like being called Benjamin. But I don't think Becky cared about what Ben liked, because she rolled her eyes and said, "Whatever, Benjamin—get in the car. We're going to be late."

Charlie and I shot each other a glance as Ben clambered into the back seat and slammed the door. And even though I knew he was going to Disney World, I felt sorry for him.

Becky honked her horn and she must have forgotten that she was angry, because her big red lips stretched into another huge smile. She shouted out the window, "Have a wonderful summer, boys!" and then, with a screech of tires, they were off.

After their car had turned the corner, Charlie did this big sigh and said, "Ben is so lucky. His new mom is really lovely."

This is what I meant by Charlie having no filter and being blurty. I glared at him and said, "Charlie, we *hate* Becky, remember?"

He puffed out his cheeks. "I know, I know, but—"

"No buts."

After that he convinced me to skip the Monster Munch and go with him to the chicken place. He said he wanted "one last supper" before he went off to Camp Mung-bean for the annual Anderson family detox. Charlie's mom turned vegan three years ago and he hasn't stopped moaning about how it has ruined his life.

He ordered a family-sized bucket at Texas Fried Chicken, and as he picked the bones clean he went on about what a lousy summer it was going to be for him at Healthy Kids = Happy Kids with only avocados to eat.

I wish I'd known at the time what was actually going to happen and then I could have put a stop to all his whining. But I didn't, so I listened to his plans to sew candy into his pajamas and hide chips in his sleeping bag, all the time thinking that my summer was going to suck waaaaaay harder than his.

2

Okay, so I warned you about the sad part. I have to tell you about it because if Grams hadn't died, then my super miraculous journey would never have happened

When I got home, I admit I wasn't in the best of moods. I think it's understandable though—I was facing the summer with no plans and no friends. As I turned the corner to my house, I saw Eileen walking Lady Gaga. When I say walking, I mean waiting with a plastic bag on her hand while Lady Gaga did her duty on the pavement. I tried to step around her, but she had this weird look on her face—Eileen, not Lady Gaga.

She tilted her head to the side and said, "You poor lamb. Now, when you're feeling strong enough you come and see me, and I'll sort out that funny haircut of yours."

I didn't know Eileen that well and I couldn't understand why she was suddenly so worried about my hair situation.

Then she dabbed her nose with a tissue and said, "I'm sorry, Fred, it was her time."

I looked at Lady Gaga and shrugged. If you gotta go, you gotta go.

Obviously now I realize Eileen wasn't talking about Lady Gaga taking a dump outside Mr. Burnley's house, but at the time I didn't think any more about it because a surprising sight had caught my eye.

That surprising sight was my dad.

He was standing at the back gate.

This was a surprising sight for two reasons.

Number one: he hadn't left the couch since his accident.

Number two: he was smoking!

I was outraged. I wasn't going to stand by while he slowly killed himself, so I shouted, "Dad! What are you doing?"

I could tell I'd surprised him because he almost toppled over. I stormed up to our house, anger fueling my legs, and immediately launched into the presentation I gave in fifth-year science on the dangers of smoking. "Dad, there are more than 5,000 chemicals in tobacco smoke—"

"You're not going to list all 5,000 now, are you, Fred?" he said in this tired-sounding voice, which I thought was a bit rude when I was trying to save his life. One dead parent is enough.

"At least 250 are known to be harmful, including hydrogen cyanide, carbon monoxide, and ammonia. And among the 250 known harmful chemicals in tobacco smoke, at least sixty-nine can cause cancer."

I could NOT believe it when he took another puff of his cigarette. I watched the smoke billowing out of his nostrils and I thought I was going to explode like the bottle of Coke at the class party.

He must have got the picture because he said, "Sorry, Fred," and dropped the butt on the ground and crushed it with his good foot.

"Why were you smoking?"

"It's your Grams."

This confused me, so I said, "Grams doesn't smoke. And, frankly, it's a bit of a low move to try and claim the cigarette *you* were smoking was hers."

"No, I don't mean that."

"What do you mean then?"

"She's gone."

I didn't know what any of this had to do with my dad's sudden nicotine habit. "Have you tried Mr. Burnley's?" I asked, because last time we couldn't find Grams she was there drinking sherry and playing strip-Monopoly. Well, she wasn't *actually* playing strip-Monopoly but she'd taken off her cardigan, so Dad and I teased her about it for weeks. But when she threatened to stop washing our underwear and baking us cakes we stopped.

"She's not at Mr. Burnley's, Fred," Dad said, shaking his head slowly. "She's *gone* gone."

"*Gone* gone?" My mind began whirling and I did *not* like the places it was going to.

"Dead, Fred. Your Grams is dead."

Just like that. That's how he said it.

I don't know why, but I laughed. Not a ha-ha-funny laugh, but a ha-ha-my-brain's-short-circuiting-and-I-have-no-control-over-my-emotions-right-now kind of laugh.

I don't know how much of what I said next Dad understood because my chin had started wobbling uncontrollably. What I wanted to say was, "How can she be dead? You said she'd outlast us all." But I think it sounded like, "Howeee. Dead. Dead. All, lastus!"

Dad sort of crumpled over the gate and said, "I'm sorry, Fred."

"Sorry? Why are you sorry? Did you kill her?" Obviously I didn't think he'd killed her—I was experiencing some sort of emotional breakdown.

"What? No!" Understandably Dad looked a little taken aback.

My throat started doing this contracting thing and

I had to keep swallowing hard so I could breathe. "Well, what happened then? She was fine when I left this morning."

"She was old, Fred. It was her time." (This was when I realized Eileen had not been talking about Lady Gaga.)

Dad reached one arm out toward me, but I took a step back. I couldn't help it. I was really, really angry and, in that moment, he was the only person I could blame.

I yelled at him. "She's always been old, but she's never died before! How could you let this happen?" I marched past him and into the house. I could hear his crutches clattering behind me.

He started shouting things like, "Stop! Fred—wait. Let's talk about this."

But I didn't stop or wait because I didn't want to hear any more words. I threw my school bag down in the hallway and stormed into the kitchen. There was this almighty crash as he tripped over my bag. I know it's wrong but a teeny part of me wanted him to have hurt himself—just a little bit—to get him back for telling me about Grams.

He wasn't hurt but he was angry. A barrage of unrepeatable words tumbled out of his mouth. Some of them I had heard before. Others—like "dunderbod"—I think he made up on the spot. It was a good job Grams was dead, because if she had heard him he'd have been in so much trouble.

"Fred! What have I told you about your school bag? Get in here now."

For a split second I considered making a run for it, but my conscience got the better of me. I walked back into the hallway at the exact moment he hurled my backpack out of the back door.

"You shouldn't have done that," I said. "There was a Capri Sun in the big pocket. It's probably burst all over my school report."

Dad didn't seem to care about that. He still looked really angry. He tried to get up, but he was a tangled mess of limbs and crutches. He swore again and launched one of his crutches and it flew out of the door and landed next to my bag. He raised his other crutch skyward, but I grabbed it before he could send it flying.

"Stop throwing stuff outside, would you?" And then I said something Grams would have said. "What would the neighbors think?"

It was then that his head dropped down and he started making this weird snorting noise, like a dying walrus. (Oooh, maybe not the best time, but I have a fact about walruses: they weigh a ton. That's as much as a car. Most people don't know that, they think they're much smaller than they are—like otter-sized—but they're massive.)

Dad wasn't mimicking the snort of a dying walrus. He was *crying*. I'd never seen him cry before but then I'd never had a dead grandmother before. I didn't know what to do so I stood there, holding on to his crutch, with my mouth open.

When eventually the snorting and sobbing had died down, he said, "Help your old man up, would you, Fred?"

I pulled him onto his good foot, then wedged myself under his armpit and maneuvered him back to the couch.

"I'm sorry, Dad." I lifted his bad leg and placed it on the footstool. "I shouldn't have left my bag there. I only did it because Grams is dead."

He let out a really big sigh and wiped his nose on the sleeve of his sweater, which he is always telling me not to do. I was going to point it out, but it didn't seem like the right moment. I'm just saying the double standard did not go unnoticed.

Dad then said, "No, *I'm* sorry, Fred. I didn't do a very good job of breaking the news. I've been thinking about how to tell you all day and then . . . well I come out with '*gone* gone.' "

This was true, he hadn't done a good job, but he looked so upset that I told him it was okay. I sat down next to him. I wasn't angry anymore. Just sad.

"How did it happen?"

"One minute she was sitting in her chair knitting and shouting at talk show repeats on the TV. The next she was gone. A stroke, they reckon." Dad looked over to Grams's empty chair. I followed his gaze. I could still see the imprint of her bottom on the seat. Her knitting was draped over the arm. I walked over and picked up the unfinished sweater. There was a rainbow-colored dinosaur on the front. I held it up for Dad to see.

He pulled a face. "Another one of her masterpieces for her favorite grandson, no doubt."

I don't feel great saying this, but I can't say I was sorry she hadn't finished that one. I hadn't been into dinosaurs for ages. I placed her knitting needles on the coffee table and we sat in silence, listening to the clock tick-tocking.

Around tick-tock number forty-six, Dad cleared his throat. "We're going to be alright, son. No matter what, okay?"

I nodded, but as I looked at his leg in plaster from ankle to hip, I wasn't convinced. The most senior person in the household was someone who had run himself over with his own mail truck.

We sat in front of the TV for the rest of the evening. Around nine o'clock I realized we hadn't eaten. I wasn't hungry, so I left Dad in the living room with a family-sized packet of onion rings and went to my bedroom to ponder. After some pondering, I headed to the bathroom, did my nighttime pee, brushed my teeth, did another little nighttime pee as I hadn't got it all out the first time, and headed back to my bedroom.

But I didn't end up there—I ended up in Grams's room. I sat on her flowery comforter and breathed in the smell of her. Lavender and mint candies.

I sat there breathing and smelling and picturing her papery wrinkles and smiling face and my heart started to hurt. I slid open a drawer of her nightstand. I wanted something of hers to have with me when I went to sleep. I thought that way I might still feel close to her.

I rummaged around through a whole heap of lottery scratch cards. I found her reading glasses, her spare set of false teeth, and a few of her hair rollers. They weren't what I had in mind as a memento, so I closed the drawer and opened the one below. Inside I spotted one of her handkerchiefs—it had little purple flowers stitched on it. I held it to my nose and as I inhaled I closed my eyes. When I opened them again, they were leaking.

3

This is where I have a proper cry and then get given a letter from Grams

The next morning Mr. Burnley came around to drive Dad into town. When someone dies there is an awful lot of paperwork to be done so that everyone knows they are really dead.

Dad had to register Grams's death and collect her death certificate. To be honest, I still don't see the point in awarding a dead person a certificate. Especially when they didn't even have to try very hard to get it. I asked Dad if he was going to put it on the wall with my gold swimming certificate. Now that *did* require effort. I had to tie knots in my pajama bottoms and blow them up to make floats while I was treading water. Dad said no—he'd have to send it to the bank. I still don't know why the bank wanted my Grams's prize for dying.

Dad told me to keep busy while he was out, so that

I wouldn't feel too sad. I logged on to my favorite fact-finding website, Factination, and learned that:

1. Bees can get drunk on alcohol, but when they return to the hive there are these bouncer bees who refuse to let them in until they sober up. Ha—funny!
2. A male swan is called a cob and the female swan is called a pen. The mute swan—the type the Queen owns—has a top speed of fifty-five miles per hour. That's the same speed Grams was going when she hit the war memorial.
3. Children's cells live on in their mothers. Babies' DNA has been found knitted into their mother's brain, bone, and heart tissue. Oh.

And that's when I stopped looking at facts. I realized that when my mom died, a tiny bit of me died too. And when Grams died, the last tiny bit of my mom died with her.

I had not reckoned on facts making me feel worse. Usually they make me feel better. After that, all I wanted to do was burrow underneath my comforter and shut out the world. I went to my closet and chose one of the sweaters Grams had made me. Once she told me she knitted me sweaters so that I had something to hug me all day. At the time I thought it was a bit cringey, but in that moment, more than anything, I needed one of her hugs.

I chose the beige one with the brown teddy bear on the front with the words *Family Makes You Happy* stitched beneath. It's important that you know I would never wear it out in public. I think I was probably using it as a sort of knitwear comfort blanket. I hid under my covers and took Grams's hanky from under my pillow and sniffed it deeply. I'm not good at crying, but it felt like one of those times when it would be worth giving it a go. I have to admit, after a few minutes of huge full-body sobs, I started feeling a little better. And then I started feeling a little hot. It was July and I was wearing a chunky knit under a comforter.

Just as I threw the covers off, I heard Dad's crutches scuffling on the carpet on the landing. He hadn't made it upstairs since the accident.

The door opened and his head poked in.

"You alright, son?" He pointed a crutch at me. "Is that one of your Grams's sweaters?"

"Uh-huh."

"Ah, that's nice. Make you feel close to her?"

"It does a little. I took a handkerchief of hers too." I held it out to him. "It smells like lavender."

Dad smiled this lopsided smile and took the hanky. It

was when he held it up that we both realized my monumental mistake.

"Oh, Freddie, you dope," he snorted. "You've been sniffing your Grams's undies."

I don't know really what to say about that other than it happened, and I've put it behind me. When Dad had regained his composure, he remembered why he'd come up to speak to me and his face became all serious.

"Fred, I've got something for you from the lawyers." He pulled out an envelope from his back pocket.

"What is it?"

His eyes started to look a little watery again, so I said, "Do you know the Chinese invented paper envelopes in the second century BC?"

And he said, "That's wonderful, Fred." Which is odd, because of all the facts I've told him in the past, I don't think this one is more wonderful than the rest.

He passed the envelope to me and I saw my name written on the front in twirly old-lady writing.

"It's from your Grams."

"But she's dead."

"She wrote it when she was alive, for you to read once she was dead."

This is also odd—if she knew she was going to die she

should have told somebody. I slid my fingers under the flap and opened it up.

Dear Fred,
My little soldier.

That was as far as I got. I suddenly felt like I might cry again, so I gulped away my tears and breathed out slowly.

Dad put his arm on my shoulder and said, "You don't have to read it now. Put it away for when you're ready. When you feel strong enough."

He tapped his cast with his crutch. "I'm going to lie down. My leg's killing me."

I helped him downstairs and onto the sofa. His voice got a little squeaky when he said, "You meant the world to your Grams. And you mean the world to me."

It felt like a bubble of sadness was ballooning in my chest, so I thought it was best if I was on my own. "I think I'm going to head upstairs to my room. Can I get you anything before I go?"

"Grab me a soda and a bag of chips, would you?"

I got him a soda and some chips and plumped up the cushions for him and then scratched a bit on his back he couldn't reach.

"You're a good boy, Fred. Your mom would be proud of you."

I never met my mom. I don't know what her voice sounded like or if she smelled of lavender like Grams or some other flower. I don't know if she could roll her tongue like I can but Dad can't, or if she got to see me before she died.

But one fact I do know about my mom is that she was easily pleased.

I mean *really* easily pleased.

I left Dad in his cloud of chips crumbs and went up to my room. I took my *Things I've Done That Would Make Mom Proud* notebook out of my desk drawer. It's where I write a list of things I have done that my dad says would have made Mom proud. There's quite a lot of entries. None of them were difficult things. But I still like reading them. Here are some examples so you get the picture.

My first day at St. Theresa's

All I accomplished was eating some Frosted Flakes and getting dressed in my uniform (I didn't even tie my shoelaces—Grams did that).

Acting in the school nativity

Not even a speaking role—I only had to wear a rubber glove strapped to my stomach as an udder and moo a couple of times.

Learning to ride my bike

Literally everyone else (other than Charlie) could ride a bike before I could.

Getting my first sticker in my math book, aged seven

I had only learned the two, five, and ten times tables. Ben had his sevens, which were really hard to get when you're in third year.

I added getting Dad a soda and some chips and the back scratching to the list as well.

I must have drifted off to sleep because when I woke up my notebook was stuck to my face with my own drool. I peeled it off carefully. A few of the words were smudged but it wasn't too bad. I couldn't believe it when I checked my robot alarm clock and it said 8 p.m.! I'd missed my dinner. Grams would never have let me miss my dinner. I need my food. I'm a growing boy.

Then I remembered Grams.

And then I remembered The Letter.

I fished it out of my back pocket and opened the flap. And that's when I saw that The Letter wasn't the only thing in the envelope. My birth certificate was also inside.

4

I should probably explain why my birth certificate led me, Charlie, and Ben on our super miraculous journey

Grams and Dad never kept it a secret. I've always known Dad isn't my biological father. My biological father left Mom when she was pregnant with me and then she met my dad not long after that. When she died just after I was born, Dad stuck around because he and Grams were all I had. I once overheard one of the dads at the school entrance say that it was a miracle that he stayed. I don't know about that. I think maybe it just makes him a really good guy.

I had only ever asked about my real father a couple of times. Grams maintained she didn't know anything about him, not even a name. Had I known she was such an accomplished liar I might have pushed her harder. Dad always looked so hurt that I stopped bringing it up.

It didn't bother me *that* much. If I'm honest, I only ever thought about my biological father if Dad and I were having an argument or when we couldn't afford something, and I wondered if my other dad might be rich.

But then, out of the blue, I had my birth certificate and I had a name.

Alan Froggley.

Yeah—not a great name.

I held off making too many judgments about Alan before I'd read Grams's letter.

Dear Fred,
My little soldier. The fact that you're reading
this means I'm probably dead.

I've left a little money for you in a bank account
for when you're eighteen. I should say to spend it on
college but I'm going to say spend it on whatever will
make you happy. And what will make you happy will
be a decent education that will set you up for life.
Don't fight me on this.

You've probably looked at your birth certificate
by now. Perhaps I should have given it to you before.
I thought about not giving it to you at all. But when
all is said and done, you have every right to know
who your biological father is. You can make up

your own mind about him, should you wish to meet
him. I'm not going to poison your mind against
that waste of space. Your real dad, Joe—he's a good
man. He became like a son to me. He was good to my
Molly when that weasel Alan left her. Joe loves you,
Freddie—with every bone of his body.

Don't forget to wear a jacket in the winter.
Pop-Tarts are not a nutritious breakfast. Remind
your dad garbage cans go out on Wednesdays.

I love you, Freddie. Always.
Don't be too sad.
Grams xxx

I was sad.

But as I lay on my bed, one name kept going around in my head.

Alan Froggley.

Alan.

Froggley.

Al.

Froggers.

I tried saying it out loud a few times, hoping it would make me feel more connected.

Alan Froggley. Alan Froggley. Alan Froggley.

It didn't work.

His name didn't conjure up anything. I held my birth certificate in my hand and thought, Who are you, Alan?

And then I saw his place of birth listed as St. David's, Wales.

Wales? Could I really be part Welsh? I can't sing a note and I'm lousy at rugby.

I don't remember making a conscious decision to look him up, but I found myself tapping *Alan Froggley* into Google. Unsurprisingly there weren't many hits. There was a story about an Alan Froggley who got his ear blown off in World War II. Definitely not him. And an Alan Froggley who lived in America and was the owner of the biggest big toes in the state of Texas. I scooched my foot out of my Incredible Hulk slipper to be sure, but if anything, my big toes were a little smaller than average. I could rule him out. The final Alan Froggley was about the right age. There was a grainy black-and-white picture on his work website. It listed him as a research analyst for a company called Cardiff Analytics. At the time I didn't know what that meant, so I googled it.

A research analyst is a professional who is responsible for reviewing, collecting, and reporting on a variety of data sets and information sources.

This basically meant he worked with facts. My stomach did the same weird wobbly thing it did every time Grams drove too fast over the hill at the bottom of the road.

I tried to see if there was a family resemblance, but I couldn't clearly make out what he looked like from the tiny photo. There was a little biography under his name that said he'd been at the company for seven years and ran a team of twelve analysts. It also said he enjoyed walking. I got excited at that because I can walk. And that he liked swimming—I've got my bronze survival award and I can swim three-quarters of a length underwater (but only with my goggles on). At this point I was convinced. Facts, walking, and swimming—it couldn't be a coincidence. I'd found him. Well, online anyway.

I still don't know where the idea to visit him in real life came from. It might have been the thought of the boring summer that was ahead of me, or that I wanted to do *something* rather than stay at home looking after Dad and missing Grams. Or it might have been because I was getting worried about the fact that my family was down to two. And if Dad kept doing things like running himself over it could end up as just me, which wasn't a good thought. But once I'd had the idea it got stuck in my head and I knew there was nothing I could do to stop it. I was going to meet my biological father.

I opened up a group chat with Ben and Charlie. I wouldn't get very far without a well-thought-out cover story and I needed their help.

F: How u doin?
C: My life sux: Mom found my secret snack stash I was hiding for Hunger Camp.
B: My life sux harder: Disney World = my own personal hell.

Ben attached a photo of his family with the cast of *Beauty and the Beast* from his Easter vacation. Becky was up front and center with her arms around Lumière. I'd never seen a candlestick look so pleased with itself. Ben was sulking at the back.

I was annoyed about their pity party, especially as I was clearly having a way worse time than them. I kind of wanted them to feel bad so I sent:

F: My life sux the most: my Grams died.

I stared at my phone, wondering how they'd reply. For a while they didn't. And then:

C: Fred wins.
B: Agreed. That does suck the most. Sorry bud.
C: Feel bad now. M8 u ok?

I got the major guilts for telling them like that.

F: Yeah, I'm ok.

There was another pause.

B: But . . . did I tell you that Becky bought us all matching T-shirts w/ I heart Mickey. That's pretty awful 2.

C: And did I mention I have 2 drink avocado & wheatgrass smoothies every morning on vegan vacation?

B: Grass? Duuuude—think we might have a new contender 4 winner of the suckiest life.

That's when I hit them with it.

F: Guys—I'm going to Wales to find my biological dad, Alan Froggley.

I'd never told them my dad wasn't my biological father. Not because I was hiding it from them, it just never came up.

C: Your biological dad is Welsh?

Yup, that's what Charlie took from that.

C: Wait! Ur biological dad?

There we go.

F: He left before I was born. But now I've found him.
B: U sure about this? What does ur actual dad think? And
how u getting there? Thought he couldnt drive.
F: Dad doesn't know. I'm going on my own. This wknd. Need
u 2 cover 4 me.

My phone told me: *Charlie is typing. Ben is typing.*
I held my breath and waited.
Then I stopped holding my breath because it was
taking them too long to reply.

F: Any1 there?

They were probably on a separate chat. Figuring out
what to say. I wished they'd hurry up.

C: I'll come wiv u. A bit of fun b4 my vegan vacay hell in
2 wks.
B: Me 2. Becky is doing my hed in. I wanna break b4 USA.
F: U sure?

I'd been secretly hoping for this outcome.

B: 👍 Don't leave for another 6 days anyways.

C: Yup.

F: Come 2 mine 2morrow 2 discuss plan?

C: Sure 10am?

F: Yup.

B: Cu 2mrrow.

5

Where Ben, Charlie, and I make a plan that, in hindsight, could have done with a teensy bit more thought

I was woken up by the sound of "We Wish You a Merry Christmas." Dad had bought one of those musical doorbells, and it had got stuck on that tune. He still hasn't fixed it because he says Christmas will be here before we know it. I think time must go quicker for adults.

Dad hollered up at me, "Get that, would you, Fred?"

I rammed my feet into my slippers and headed downstairs. Dad craned his neck to look at me through the living-room door. "Hey, bedhead, thought I'd let you lie in. Reckon you needed your sleep." He held out a package of chocolate cookies. I shook my head—what would Grams say if I started my day with a cookie?

"You seen this?" Dad nodded toward the TV. "This absolute joker stole some priceless rings right from under Fiona Bruce's nose."

"Who?" On the screen was a woman with excellent teeth looking very dismayed.

"From the *Antiques Roadshow*—Fiona Bruce. Some thief in a ski cap swiped these rings live on the air off this poor old dear. Disappeared without a trace."

To be honest, I wasn't giving Dad my full attention. Antiques weren't really my thing. "I'm going to answer the door."

Ben and Charlie were on the doorstep with their arms over each other's shoulders, swaying from side to side.

"And a happy New Year!" They finished the song and took a bow. Ben took his baseball cap off and held it out for money.

I felt a little emotional when I saw them. I didn't want to cry so I said, "Did you know Joseph Henry invented the doorbell in 1831?" and the tears stopped prickling the back of my eyeballs.

Charlie at least looked impressed. "I did not know that."

Ben was not distracted by the doorbell fact. He did this concerned frown and said, "You alright, Fred?"

"Course he's not alright, he's in the middle of a personal crisis." Charlie pushed past me and marched into the living room. Dad was still watching the news. There was a picture of two gold rings shaped like swans on the screen and the word *REWARD*. Dad muted the TV. "Morning, boys."

Charlie cleared his throat. "Mom says I'm to say sorry, Mr. Yates. About your . . ." He paused. "What was Freddie's Grams to you? She was Freddie's mom's mom, right? So that makes her your dead girlfriend's mom?"

Dad blinked twice at Charlie then looked at me. I shrugged—what could I say?

Charlie tried again. "Mr. Yates. I am very sorry to hear that your dead girlfriend's mom is also dead too." He looked at the chocolate cookie that Dad was holding below his open mouth. "You going to eat that?"

Dad handed the cookie over and said, very slowly, "Thank you for your heartfelt condolences, Charlie."

"You are very welcome, Mr. Yates."

"How's your leg, Mr. Yates?" Ben asked.

"Getting better, thanks. Few more weeks in the cast though."

"Mom says you'd have to be pretty special to run yourself over with your own car." Charlie's lips spread into a huge grin until Ben nudged him in the ribs.

"What?" Charlie glared at Ben. "I was paying him a compliment."

Dad sighed. "How's your mom, Ben? She okay after everything?"

"She's living in Spain. Wants to be as far away from Dad and Becky as possible. She doesn't understand why Dad waited until she left him to get rich. Thinks he did it to spite her."

"Right." Dad ran his hands through his hair and it stuck up like a mad professor's. "Can you win five hundred grand on a scratch card out of spite?"

"Mom seems to think so."

"Shall we go up to my room?" I wanted to get on with making our plan—not stand around all day talking to Dad.

Charlie sat on my desk chair and put his big feet on my bed. "So you've got two dads?"

"Yup—my proper dad and my biological dad who lives in Wales."

"Where even is Wales? Is it one of them islands between here and France?"

Mrs. Walker had been right about Charlie needing to pay more attention in class.

Ben set him straight. "No, you muppet. It's that bit stuck to us that looks like a pig's head."

"*There?* How are we going to get there?"

"On the train." I brought up the train schedule on my computer. "But it isn't cheap. How much money have you guys got?"

Charlie turned out the pockets of his cargo pants. "I've got four pounds and sixteen pence."

"That's not enough."

I had my life savings stored in my Kermit money jar. I pulled out the stopper and a shower of silver and brown coins fell onto the carpet. It looked like loads.

I noticed Ben was smirking. I scowled at him. "What?"

"Dude, you've been saving your money in a Kermit money jar."

"So?"

"Kermit? And now you find out your biological dad's name is *Froggley*. It's a little funny, that's all."

I didn't think it was funny—and even though I didn't believe in them at the time, I thought it was a sign. A sign, mind you, not a miracle.

It started to feel like less of a sign when I counted out the coins and they totaled £8.53. "That makes twelve pounds something. That's not going to get us to Wales."

I didn't want to appear presumptuous, but I looked straight at Ben. I *may* have been banking on his monetary input all along, but I was trying to be subtle about it. I was hoping to lead him to make the offer of financial aid himself.

Charlie, on the other hand, was not subtle about it. He prodded Ben with his foot and said, "Come on, moneybags, hand over the cash."

Ben looked uncomfortable. Ever since his dad got rich, he has this thing about people using him for his money. He does get more allowance than me and Charlie combined though.

"He doesn't have to if he doesn't want to," I said, but I didn't mean it. I was doing what they call a double bluff. Or maybe it's a single bluff. I'm not sure.

"Go on, Ben, cough up. His Grams died, and I've always wanted to go to Wales."

"You didn't know where Wales was two minutes ago."

There was this awkward moment when nobody spoke, and I thought Ben might not pay up, but then he said, "Fine. Sorry—yes. Course I'll put in some money."

"I'll pay you back, I promise." Note that I did not commit myself to a timeline.

After we sorted out the money, we discussed our cover story. I suggested we could say we'd won a prize trip, but that got too complicated. Charlie thought we could leave a ransom note and pretend we'd all been kidnapped, but we thought our parents might get too overexcited about that. In the end we opted for Ben's idea: I'd say I was staying at Ben's. Ben would say he was staying at Charlie's, and Charlie would say he was staying at mine. Ben said it was genius in its simplicity.

As it turned out, our parents were quite relaxed about it all to begin with. I thought Dad would see straight through me because I have a very honest face. But when I said, "Dad, I'm going to sleep over at Ben's. I'll be back Sunday," he said:

"Where's the remote?"

Now, after everything that happened, he makes me leave him a full itinerary of what I'm up to whenever I go out. He even looked into getting me electronically chipped like Lady Gaga—the dog, not the singer (I've no idea if she's tagged).

Ben, Charlie, and I agreed to meet at the bus stop at eight the following morning. We decided to pack light—a spare pair of underwear and a few snacks to keep us going. At that point I guess I assumed that my new dad, Alan, would put us up, and we'd only be away for a night. When people ask me if I would do anything differently in my journey if I were to do it all again, I tell them I would take more underpants. More clothes in general really.

6

I guess this is the beginning of our super miraculous journey

Because of all the excitement churning in my belly, I woke up really early. I tried staying in bed but there was no way I was getting back to sleep. I packed my best boxer shorts into my bag. I remember thinking that the next time I put them on I would have met Alan Froggley. Interestingly, the first men's underwear worn 7,000 years ago (!) took the form of the leather loincloth. We don't wear leather underwear anymore because the immense sweat buildup wasn't fun for anybody's nether regions.

I tiptoed past the living room, which Dad had claimed as his bedroom ever since his accident. He was on the couch, snoring, his face illuminated by the blue glow from the TV. I knew I should have breakfast even though I was feeling excited-sick. I picked up a box of Pop-Tarts but put them back when I remembered Grams's letter and opted for Shredded Wheat instead.

Just after seven o'clock I reckoned it would be okay to head over to the bus stop near Ben's. I didn't know whether to wake Dad or not. I stood over him, watching the rise and fall of his chest. He looked so peaceful. I wanted to wrap my arms around him like I used to when I was little. It was quite a nice moment until he suddenly bolted upright and swung at me with one of his crutches. I was so surprised I peed a little in my boxers.

I screamed. He screamed. We both screamed.

"Fred! What the hell are you doing? I thought you were an intruder!"

"I was watching you sleep!"

"Holy smoke, why were you doing that, son? You could have given me a heart attack."

"You're the one wielding your crutch!"

"Fred, watching someone sleep is just plain creepy. Don't do it again."

He had a point.

"I came to say goodbye. I'm off to Ben's."

He rubbed his stubble. Every day he was looking more and more crusty. "What time is it?"

"Just after seven."

"For the love of all things bright and beautiful, Fred. What're you doing up so early?"

"It's not that early."

"It is for me."

He was right about that. He hadn't been up much before eleven most mornings since he was laid off from work. "When're you back?"

"Tomorrow evening."

He stretched out his arms and did a huge yawn that sounded like an angry dinosaur. Dad always does these really noisy yawns. "Be a good boy, make me a cup of tea before you go."

I gave Dad his tea and he told me Mom would be proud. I didn't need to write that in my book though, because I already had it down. Dad drinks a lot of tea. In fact, I only ever see him drink one of two liquids—tea or soda.

"I'll see you later then, Dad."

"Have fun. Behave yourself."

I paused in the doorway. The moment didn't feel quite big enough somehow. "I love you. And I promise I'll be back soon. Don't worry, okay?"

Dad's forehead went all crinkly. "Everything alright, Fred?"

Maybe I'd said too much. I was only supposed to be going to Ben's. I thought I might have given the game away, but then he said, "Sorry, of course it's not alright. I know how much you miss your Grams. And it's not going to be much of a summer for you with me laid up like this."

I had to squeeze my lips together to stop myself from

blurting out that I was sneaking off to Wales in search of Alan Froggley. I usually told Dad everything. But I couldn't tell him that I was off to secure myself a backup father. He might not let me go.

And also, I couldn't bring myself to hurt him like that.

When I got to the bus stop I was surprised to see that Ben was already there. The bus wasn't due for another half hour.

"Becky wanted me to join in with some family mindful meditation yoga thing. I had to get out of there," he explained. "She made Dad wear this Lycra outfit."

I pulled a face. Trust me, you don't want to see Ben's dad in stretchy material.

"I know, right? It was practically a leotard. When he dropped into this low squat pose, I left."

It was a good move on Ben's part. No one should have to witness that.

"They bought it then—that you're staying at Charlie's?"

"Oh yeah. Don't think Dad was listening, to be honest." Ben looked behind me. "Speaking of Charlie . . ."

Charlie rocked up with a Mars Bar in each hand and his hypoallergenic pillow under one arm.

"Hungry?" Ben asked.

"Storing up before the Anderson clan depart for Camp Stomach Cramp." By the time the bus arrived, Charlie was two chocolate bars down and we were surrounded by a gaggle of geriatrics from Grams's book club. I was worried they might be suspicious and ask where we were going, but they were too pumped up about their morning Zumba class to notice us. Then one of them called Doreen recognized me. After that they spent the rest of the journey sighing and looking at me with their sad wrinkly eyes. They all said that Grams was a wonderful person. Doreen was particularly gushing about her and gave us each twenty pence and told us not to spend it all at once. I remembered Grams talking about a Doreen. They'd had an argument in the supermarket over a discounted ham. Grams wasn't as generous in her comments. I think she'd said something like, "She'd drink tea with the devil, that one."

When we got to the train station I began to get The Nerves big-time. Dad was at home with only one working leg and no one to fetch him a cup of tea. I didn't feel like a very responsible son. In fact, I felt like a traitor.

Ben was a bit dismissive when I mentioned this. He said, "Your dad can manage for one night without a cup of tea." Then he told us to wait by the garbage bins and not wander off while he bought the tickets. He was quite forceful about it. I think he was enjoying being in charge for once. I would have said something, but I sensed it would be a bad idea to upset *the money*.

Getting onto the correct train passed without incident—apart from Charlie getting stuck in the station gates. He dropped his ticket and got squashed between the automatic barriers. The guard said, "I've never seen anyone do that in thirteen years." Charlie looked a little proud about that.

When the doors to the train closed and we began to chug out of the station, The Nerves came back with renewed force. "Maybe we should get off at the next stop and turn around and go back."

Ben did not like this idea. He used a very stern voice. "We're going to Cardiff, Freddie. It's not all about you."

I was confused by that, because I'd thought it was. But it turned out that Ben wanted to get away from his family as much as I wanted to find mine.

7

We manage to find Cardiff Analytics— you didn't think we would, did you?

When we arrived at the Cardiff station we went to Burger King because Charlie needed cheering up. He'd left his hypoallergenic pillow on the train. He reckoned this was down to his blood sugar having dipped to dangerously low levels. He's not at his best when he's hungry, so we decided we needed to get some food into him fast. He ordered his Whopper meal in a strong Welsh accent, which was a surprise to me and Ben.

The girl with the stenciled-on eyebrows didn't look impressed. She said, "Are you disrespecting me?"

Ben said, "Sorry, he's a bit overexcited."

After we had sat down at the plastic table, we asked Charlie why he had done it.

He said, "I have a very suggestable ear for accents."

"We've been here less than five minutes."

"What can I say? It's a talent."

I worked out that Cardiff Analytics was within walking distance of the station. We followed the little blue dot on Google Maps and twenty minutes and one pee stop later we were outside the revolving doors of Alan Froggley's office. I couldn't believe it had been so easy. I was beginning to think a career as a private investigator might be for me.

"You ready?" Ben asked.

"Yes," I said, even though I suddenly wasn't sure if I was. My whole body was nervous.

Ben must have noticed because he said, "You want us to come in with you?"

I did but I said, "No, it's alright," because I thought it was probably something I should do on my own. And I couldn't trust Charlie not to use his bad Welsh accent again.

Ben said, "Good luck, Fred," with such a serious expression it made me feel even more nervous.

Charlie pulled me in for a hug. He smelled faintly of pickles and ketchup. "You'll be grand, so you will." Charlie's sensitive ear for accents wasn't so sensitive that he could tell the difference between Welsh and Irish.

I stepped into the revolving door and shuffled around very slowly. Ben and Charlie waved the entire time—even when it had become awkward to keep waving. They only stopped when I completed a full revolution and stepped back outside again.

"What are you doing?" Ben folded his arms.

"He's chickened out, so he has," Charlie said.

Charlie was right. The doubt was creeping up through my body. What if he didn't want anything to do with me? What then? I didn't think I could take another emotional blow.

Ben pointed at the door. "Get back in there. Those train tickets cost me fifty-four quid."

I wasn't sure I liked Ben's newfound bossy side, but he looked like he meant business, so I stepped back into the revolving door. Before I started the slow shuffle around, Ben shouted, "Don't worry, dude, he's going to love you."

I really hoped he was right.

As I walked into the large entrance foyer, a security guard with quite a substantial mustache looked me up and down and said, "This isn't a playground." Which I thought was a strange thing to say as we were obviously in an office.

I hurried past him to the reception desk where a lady with a big face and an even bigger mouth was clicking her long sparkly nails on a computer keyboard. Her lips stretched into a smile when she spotted me, but her voice was clipped. "Hello, how can I help you?" is what she said, but her eyes said, *Why are you here bothering me, kid?*

I puffed up my chest and tried to sound confident. "I'm here to see Alan Froggley."

"And how are you spelling that?"

"A L A—"

"I meant the Froggley part. Two gs or one?"

"Two. F R O G G L E Y."

Her sparkly nails clicked her keyboard some more. The way she was hammering the keys made me think I might have annoyed her with the A L A N thing.

"I'm sorry, we don't have an Alan Froggley at Cardiff Analytics. Is there anything else I can help you with?"

All the puff seeped out of my chest.

"Are you absolutely sure? Did you spell Alan right?"

She stared at me for a whole minute without blinking and then said, in a surprisingly cheerful voice, "There is no Alan—spelled A L A N—Froggley at Cardiff Analytics."

"He's on your website."

"I'm sorry, we don't have an Alan Froggley."

"He enjoys walking and swimming."

She smiled again. "Is there anything else I can help you with?"

"But it says he works here—on the internet. I saw him!" I accidently shouted that bit, but Big Face didn't flinch.

Her smile became a little thinner, but she said the

exact same thing again: "I'm sorry, we don't have an Alan Froggley at Cardiff Analytics. Is there anything else I can help you with?"

"But I've come all the way from Andover."

And this is when Big-Face-Sparkly-Nails snapped. She leaned toward me and hissed, "Now listen here, you little twerp. I said we don't have an Alan Froggley working here. Now stop pestering me and go away."

I was a little shocked, so I didn't move. This was not how things were supposed to go.

"Scoot." She looked over at the guard. "Nigel, see him out."

The mustachioed security guard took a step toward me. I knew that if I didn't leave I'd be in trouble, but I wasn't sure if Big Face was telling the truth. I'd made it all the way to Cardiff—I'd even made it through the revolving doors. The thought of leaving and knowing nothing about Alan was suddenly too much to bear. I had to do something.

I contemplated making a dash for it and shouting out Alan's name down the corridors. I must have had a look of rebellion about me because Nigel lurched forward and grabbed my arm before I could get out my first cry of "Alan Froggley, where are you?"

"Now I've got you," he said, and he lifted me off the ground!

"You can't do this!"

"Looks like I can."

I pedaled my legs like mad, but he wouldn't let go. He was determined he was going to carry me out.

I looked outside for some support from my friends, but they were waving sticks around like lightsabers and were too deeply involved in their battle to notice. Panic took hold of me. Cardiff Analytics was my only lead to Alan Froggley—they couldn't throw me out. I had to do something.

"Out you go." Nigel started to push me into the revolving doors.

"No," I said, and I can't say that I'm one hundred percent proud of what I did next, but I dropped to the floor, wrapped myself around his legs, and began to beg.

"I will not leave until somebody gives me the information. Somebody must know something! Please tell me." Turns out I can yell quite loudly when motivated.

Nigel tried to shake me off, but I clung on tight. Grams always said I could be dogged when I put my mind to something.

"Get off!"

"Not until you reveal the truth about where he is. What is this company hiding?"

Nigel began hopping around the foyer, but I did not let go.

"I'm not leaving until someone tells me what happened to Alan Froggley. I beg of you."

Big-Face-Sparkly-Nails suddenly hollered over, "You alright there, Nigel? Want me to call security?"

"I *am* security, Tiffany. And I think I can handle some mixed-up kid."

I loosened my grip a little. What if I *was* just some mixed-up kid? Maybe I'd made a massive mistake, maybe I'd got it all wrong.

But then Nigel stopped hopping and said, "Did you say Alan Froggley?"

I looked up at him. "Yes, Alan Froggley, who enjoys walking and swimming—where is he?"

He stared down at me. "I knew Alan Froggley. He left here over two years ago. Personal reasons."

"You knew him?" I was actually talking to someone who knew my biological dad.

"We weren't like friends or anything, but yeah—I knew Al."

"Al? He called himself Al." I let go of Nigel's leg and slid onto the floor. "Where did he go?"

Nigel crouched down next to me and I saw that he had friendly eyes. "What's all this about, kid?"

I didn't want to get into a deep and meaningful discussion, so I said, "I need to find him, that's all."

"Think he was headed back home."

"Do you know where that is?"

Nigel stroked his top lip. "Sorry, son."

But Nigel didn't need to be sorry because I'd worked it out. I'd seen Al's registered place of birth on my birth certificate—I knew where his home was. I jumped to my feet. "Thanks, Nigel."

"Hey, kid, you alright?" he called after me.

"Yes, Nigel. I'm alright. I'm more than alright."

And then I stopped.

"Did he look like me?"

Nigel's face crumpled into a frown and then he said, "Yeah, kid, he did a bit."

I felt my heart do this little flutter in my chest.

I marched outside, and Charlie and Ben lowered their weapons.

"That was quick."

"He's not here. We're off."

They exchanged worried glances.

But I was too inspired to worry about worried glances, so I said, "Don't just stand there—follow me!"

"Why, where are we going?" Charlie asked.

"St. David's. The birthplace of Alan Froggley."

8

Our journey to St. David's continues (with a detour at Barry for some onions)

As none of us knew where St. David's was, I googled it. "Looks like St. David's is on the most western part of Wales. It says here that it is the final resting place of the patron saint of Wales, St. David."

Charlie pulled a packet of bacon chips out of his back pocket but paused before he opened them. "What are the chances of that—finally resting in a place that has your name? Makes me want to stay clear of anywhere called St. Charlie."

Ben set him straight: "I think it was named *after* he finally rested there, doofus."

Charlie put a bacon chip most of the way into his mouth, then pulled it out and said, "So he's still resting there now, this Saint David?"

"I dunno, probably. Let's find out," I said and marched off in the direction of the train station.

"You seem pumped," Charlie said, running after me.

"I am pumped."

Then Ben said, "How are you planning to pay for the tickets, Fred?" and that completely depumped me. I was obviously not thinking *I* would pay, I was thinking *he* would. "I was hoping—"

He butted in before I could start begging. "Because I don't have any cash left."

And that put the kibosh on that plan.

"Where's all the money gone?"

"Feeding you two," Ben said. "I only brought eighty quid and most of that's gone on the tickets here and lunch and snacks. A lot of snacks."

This was not ideal information to hear. "How much have we got left? Let's get as far as we can on that."

"About eleven quid."

That wasn't a lot.

"What are we going to do?" Charlie asked a bacon chip.

I put my hands on my hips. "Buses are cheaper. We might be able to get there by bus."

So that was the extent of our plan—we'd get a bus to St. David's.

It didn't take long for us to find a bus stop. We didn't know what number we needed, but I figured we'd wait for the first bus to come along and see where it was going. I hoped for a miracle that it might be going straight there, but my miracle didn't happen in Cardiff.

Just as Charlie had finished his chips a number 96A bus pulled up and opened its doors.

"We want to go to St. David's."

"You won't be going to St. David's on this bus."

"Where's this bus go?"

"I'm driving to Barry."

"Well, where's Barry going to then?"

"Barry isn't going anywhere, boyo! Barry's a place."

Charlie leaned in. "Is it named after a Barry?"

"Maybe."

"Is he still resting there too?"

"I've got a busy day, what with Barry's festival. Are you getting on or not?"

"That depends," I said. "Is Barry closer to St. David's than here?"

"I suppose—"

"In that case, three tickets to Barry, please, driver."

I fidgeted the whole journey. Grams would have told me I was like a ferret in a sock, but it was impossible to calm my brain down. I couldn't stop thinking about what I should say to Alan when I met him. If I met him. I mean, there was still no guarantee I'd actually find him. But I'd already started imagining him as a kind of reserve dad, I guess. In case of emergencies. I probably wouldn't sell it to him as a backup position though. No one wants to be on the bench. But then maybe he wouldn't want to be on the field either.

In all honesty, my head was a jumble and I was still no clearer about things when we arrived at the last stop, Barry Docks.

It had turned out to be a nice day and as I watched the little boats bobbing about in the water, my muddled head began to clear and I actually started to feel a little more optimistic, despite our financial situation. It had cost us a fiver to get to Barry from Cardiff. It would have been more, but Ben had haggled the driver down by promising that we'd clear all the rubbish off the bus floor. He's quite entrepreneurial like that. But even with the discount I knew we were going to struggle to get much farther without a serious cash injection. Which was why it was lucky for us that Charlie found a flyer hidden under a crumpled copy of the *Barry Gazette*.

"I could do this," Charlie said, waving the flyer in the air.

"Do what?" Ben asked.

"This—I reckon I could win it, easy."

I took the piece of paper he was holding and read it out

loud: "Barry's Annual Onion-Eating Competition—the highlight of Barry Festival."

"I might not be a runner or a soccer player, I can't even swim that well, but this—this I could win." There was something about Charlie's big excited eyes that made me think he really could.

Ben snorted. "Onion eating? Who wants to eat an onion?"

"Someone who wants to win fifty pounds," I said.

That got Ben's interest.

"Give me that. Fifty quid to eat an onion?"

"And onions are a very good source of vitamin C. They are also close relatives of the leek, chive, and garlic," I said, because I had just remembered those facts.

"Can a vegetable have relatives?" Charlie asked.

Ben grinned. "Well, you do."

I pointed at the flyer. "Says here that to win you have to eat one onion faster than anyone else. You really reckon you could do it, Charlie?"

Charlie shrugged. "Easy money. I was born for this."

The driver, who was having a cigarette outside in the sun (despite my impassioned warning regarding the 5,000 chemicals he was inhaling), must have been eavesdropping on our conversation because he said, "There's nothing easy about eating raw onions."

Ben said, "I don't want to be disrespectful, Mr. Bus Driver, sir, but really—*how hard can it be?*"

Turns out very hard.

On the walk from the docks to the park we realized that the Barry Festival was a really big deal to the people of Barry. The place was swarming. Banners hung from streetlights; we passed three ice-cream trucks and a band of bearded old men playing country music on banjos. For some reason we still can't work out, the trees and road signs had been covered with colorful knitting.

We followed the crowds to where the onion-eating competition was being held. Charlie remained admirably confident about his chances. This was despite spotting an enormous man who was wearing cowboy boots and a massive belt—the type that prize-winning boxers wear. But instead of boxing logos, this belt was decorated with three metal onions. We later found out that his name was Big Trev and he was the reigning champion.

A stage had been erected in the middle of the green. We had to pay fifty pence each and give our names to a lady wearing a T-shirt that said, *What do you make with onions and beans?* on the front. I considered this for a while but when she turned around the answer was on the back. It was *Tear gas.* We all thought that was very funny.

While we waited for the competition to start, we had

a look around the booths. Ben and I turned down all the free samples of onion-based products to make sure we had an empty stomach for the competition.

"No sense in filling ourselves up," Ben said.

Charlie was not of the same opinion. He went for it. He tried onion jams, chutneys, marmalades, *jelly*. Even onion-flavored ice cream. At the time I thought he might be killing his chances, but it turned out that Charlie had the right idea. All the sampling had a twofold positive effect.

1. His taste buds were acclimated.
2. His stomach was lined.

Ben and I were about to find out the hard way that professional onion eaters never compete on a completely empty stomach.

Once we'd been around the booths, we took a look at the entrants for the scarecrow competition, which was Sunday's big event. I thought they'd be nothing, but they were actually quite good. There was a SpongeBob SquarePants scarecrow and one that was supposed to be a guy called Tom Jones, who is apparently some famous Welsh singer. Our favorite entry was three scarecrows dressed as superheroes. We took a selfie in front of Spiderman, Batman, and Supergirl.

After that we listened to an old man playing a keyboard. His name was Keyboard Keith and he was pretty funny. He kept replacing the words of famous songs with onion-themed lyrics. For example, Lady Gaga's song "Poker Face" was changed to "Onion Face." It was hilarious, and it didn't take long before we joined in really loudly. The Welsh certainly know how to have a good time.

When he finished, a hush fell over the crowd as a group of anxious-looking people appeared on the stage to arrange some onions on long tables. I had never seen anything like it. They were humongous. The onions, not the people. Ben nudged me, Charlie gasped, and I wondered what we had got ourselves into.

"There's no way I'm going to manage to eat a raw onion the size of a soccer ball. Fifty quid or no fifty quid," I said.

Ben let out a long, low whistle and then said, "I've never seen onions like those."

Charlie stretched his neck to one side, then the other, then cracked his knuckles. "Don't worry, guys, I've got this covered."

We all breathed a sigh of relief when Keyboard Keith explained that the judging of the largest onion competition was about to start. Following a very lengthy deliberation to decide the winner between Dyllis's onion, which was the tallest, or Eric's onion, which had a greater mass, a somewhat anticlimactic tie was announced.

Keyboard Keith then took to the microphone again and invited all those involved in the main event—the onion-eating competition—to come on up.

Charlie rolled his shoulders and jumped on the spot a couple of times. "Let's go! I'm hungry and I'm hungry for onion."

Ben and I followed behind with distinctly less enthusiasm.

There were three rows of tables. Big Trev got to sit right in the middle of the front row on a special seat that had been decorated with plastic gold onions to make it look like a throne. We were in the back row with the other debut onion eaters. A lady came along and put a paper plate in front of each contestant. Another woman followed her with a basket and put a peeled onion on each plate.

Ben, who was sitting on my left, started speaking to his onion. He kept saying, "You're just an onion, I can eat you. For fifty quid, I can eat you."

I don't think the onion was any more convinced than I was. I picked up my onion and sniffed it—just to get a sense of what I was dealing with—but was quickly shouted at by the basket woman.

"No touching until *he* finishes the fanfare."

I looked where she was pointing and saw that *he* was Keyboard Keith. He was holding up a trumpet with a little flag dangling from it. The flag was embroidered with an onion motif. Barry really had gone to town on this event.

After Keith had finished quite a long trumpet solo, children from the scout troop of Barry lined up, one behind each competitor. Each scout was armed with a stopwatch.

"Competitors, raise your onions to your mouths," Keyboard Keith declared. "But do not begin eating until I give the command."

"What's the command?" Ben asked.

Keith scowled. "The command is to eat."

Big Trev must have misunderstood, because he took a bite of his onion. The crowd gasped. Charlie and I looked at each other. Something bad had happened.

Keith blew angrily into his trumpet and then shouted, "Disqualified!"

Big Trev was instantly on his feet, shouting, "You said eat!"

"I didn't."

"You did actually," Ben said, looking a bit like he was enjoying himself.

"I was explaining the procedure because *you* asked," Keith said, waving his trumpet in Ben's direction.

"It's not my fault. I asked a legitimate question. He's the one who bit his onion. Nobody made him."

Big Trev rounded on Ben. Things were getting tense

up there onstage. "I'm the reigning champion of Barry's onion-eating competition."

"Not anymore you're not," Ben said matter-of-factly.

I was convinced Big Trev was going to flatten him.

But he didn't. Instead he turned around with a look of desperation on his face and threw himself at Keith's mercy.

"Can't I have another onion?"

"You know the rules."

Big Trev slumped into his chair. "No. No. No. It can't end like this. I was on course for a four-year streak—that's never been done before."

Keith patted Trev's shoulder twice. "Come on now, pal, don't make a spectacle of yourself. The rules can't be broken. You took a bite before the command was given. Now, please leave the stage."

Murmurs rippled through the crowd. Big Trev looked like he might explode. There were a few heckles of "Give him a chance, Keith." But Keith would not be swayed. Eventually, Big Trev removed his prize belt, kissed it, and placed it on the table. He then took a slow bow and left the stage, while making the slit-throat sign at Ben.

As everyone else felt the awkward silence wash over them, Ben whispered to Charlie, "It's down to you now. That's your main opponent dispatched."

He then leaned over to me and said, "The fifty quid is as good as ours."

To this day I don't know whether Ben had planned to sabotage Big Trev's record attempt. I never thought of him as that sort.

I looked over at Charlie, who was performing a few last-minute warm-up lunges, and realized something. All that stood in the way of continuing our journey to find Alan was Charlie's ability to eat an onion faster than the residents of Barry. If I'm honest, it wasn't the most reassuring of realizations.

9

This is where we all eat raw onions.
Spoiler alert: they taste rank

I'm not a huge fan of vegetables, so chomping through an onion was always going to be a challenge. I ate raw onion once before by accident. It was hiding in a plate of fried shrimp. It was red and I didn't know what it was. It ruined my trip to my favorite restaurant and I vowed never to eat raw onion again. But there I was, on a stage in Wales, facing a glistening white orb. I was prepared to try—for the bus fare to get me to St. David's final resting place. And hopefully to Alan Froggley.

Keith gave the command. "Competitors, raise your onions."

Ben bashed his onion into mine and said, "Cheers."

I swallowed hard. My mouth knew what was coming because it began to fill with saliva.

Keith bowed at all us competitors, turned to face the audience, and bellowed, "Eat."

Nobody moved in case they'd misheard.

Keith said, "Well, what are you waiting for? Eat!" And then did another little toot on his trumpet.

We were off!

I took a breath, closed my eyes, and sank my teeth into the onion. For a split second it was okay. In fact, the first crunch was quite satisfying. But as I began to chew, my nose got very hot and my tongue began to tingle. And then my tongue began to throb. My lips pulsated. I began to sweat. My vision became blurred because my eyes streamed. Then my nose started to run. Saliva pooled out of the side of my mouth. My whole body was leaking.

It is a well-known fact that the average human child's body is sixty-five percent water. I reckon halfway through my first mouthful of onion, I was down to under thirty-five percent.

Another well-known fact is that raw onion is disgusting.

I wasn't the only one in onion hell—Ben was struggling too. Like me, he was a snotting, dribbling, crying mess. His eyes were bloodshot and his face was bright red. He gave me a look of such desperation that I wanted to tell him it was okay, he'd tried and he could stop if he wanted to.

Charlie was faring much better. He was plowing

through his onion like it was a chocolate orange. He had this look of utter determination in his eyes. He really wanted that win. And I wanted it too. More for him than the money.

I glanced around at the other competitors. Ben and I, at only two bites in, were well out of the running. It was now between Charlie, a tangerine-orange crinkly-faced woman with toilet paper stuffed up each nostril, and a skinny man in a shiny green jacket.

They all had very different techniques. Charlie was going for the chomp and chew. The orange-skinned lady was nibbling it very quickly and spinning it around in her hands like corn on the cob. The skinny man put the *whole* thing in his mouth at once and was working his way through it. He looked like a snake swallowing an egg.

Anyway, it was all very close. Charlie and the orange lady—who I now know is called Clementine!—raised their hands and opened their mouths almost at the same time to show they had finished. If I'm honest, I think she might have clinched it. Snakey-thin man finished a fraction after them both.

Keith blew on his trumpet and Ben and I dropped our half-eaten onions down on our plates and groaned. My belly was already complaining about the evilness I was making it digest. The lady in the tear-gas T-shirt hurried onto the stage and whispered in Keith's ear.

When I say whisper, it was a loud sort of angry whisper so that everyone on the stage could just about hear what she was saying. I think she said, "We can't have another draw—not after the largest onion competition. We need a winner." She glared at Keith and jabbed her finger at her clipboard, then she looked over at Charlie and Clementine and raised her eyebrows very meaningfully.

Keith must have got the message because he nodded somewhat solemnly, then announced to the crowd: "It was a closely fought battle here today at Barry's 114th Onion-Eating Competition. A 'well done' to all the competitors . . . but there can only be one winner."

Charlie wiped his mouth on his T-shirt and gave the orange lady a sideways look. He must have been thinking the same as me—she'd got in there before him. The fifty quid didn't look like it would be coming to us. This was completely disappointing.

"There has been another disqualification." Keith tugged at his collar and waited for the gasps and grumbles from the crowd to die down. "According to rule sixteen, section 1.2a, contestants may not use any of the following: goggles or masks to cover the eyes, pegs or clips on the nose, or any material inserted into one or both nostrils."

Clementine tried discreetly to remove the toilet paper stuffed up her nose, but she was onstage in front of the whole of Barry. It wasn't going to go unnoticed.

"This means I am pleased to announce that"—Keith checked the piece of paper that he'd been handed— "Charlie Anderson is the 114th winner of Barry's Onion-Eating Competition."

This was totally the opposite of disappointing! I'm not big on rules, but rule sixteen, section 1.2a, is a particularly good one. In fact, in that moment, it was my favorite rule of all time.

Charlie looked like he couldn't believe it at first.

Ben had to say, "Charlie, dude, you did it—you won."

Charlie's whole face stretched into this huge smile. He punched the air, pulled his T-shirt over his head and started running around the stage like he'd just scored the winning goal in the World Cup final. To be fair to him, the people of Barry were cheering like it was the World Cup final.

Afterward he said to me, "I never thought I'd find out what winning felt like."

10

Where we try and convince Charlie it is a good idea to stay in Barry for the night and he falls for it

Charlie was given his cash prize in an envelope and a bunch of onion-based products in a wicker basket. Honestly, I can't remember a time he'd ever looked so happy. I had to break it to him that it wouldn't be practical to carry the basket all the way to St. David's. He said he'd had enough of onions for a while anyway, so he took the cheese-and-onion chips but gave the rest to Clementine. She turned out to be Big Trev's mom and the gesture served to smooth over some of the bad feeling.

"It was a well-fought match," she said, taking the basket. "I'm sorry things got tricky back there with my Trevor. He's a good boy. Just has a terrible temper sometimes. Shouldn't dwell. I have to move on and focus on the scarecrow competition. Trevor and I worked night and day on our entry."

"Which one is yours?" I asked.

"Ones," she said with a knowing smile. "We did the superheroes."

"That's our favorite!" I reckoned they stood a good chance of winning.

By the time Charlie had his photo taken for the *Barry Gazette* it was getting late. In all the excitement we'd forgotten that we were working in a limited time frame and my anxiety levels were rising. We all called home to let our parents know everything was okay and to keep them from getting suspicious, and then we headed back to the bus stop. But when we got back to Barry Docks there wasn't any sign of a bus. We checked out the South Wales bus schedule on our phones and discovered that, at six thirty, we weren't going to make it to St. David's. So we wouldn't be staying at Alan's. Essentially, we were stuck in Barry.

Charlie did not take this information well. In fact, he behaved like a total diva. Just goes to show how quickly one moment in the limelight can affect some people.

"What are we going to do? Mom says *I* need a full night's sleep in a proper bed, or I won't be at my perkiest in the morning." Charlie said *I* in a very self-important way.

"We could hitch a lift to St. David's and still stay at Fred's new dad's?" Ben suggested.

"No way—we could be picked up by a murderer or a crazed fan."

I agreed with Charlie that I did not want our trip to come to murder, but Ben seemed to be taking a far more relaxed view to stranger danger because he said, "I think the chances of that are pretty slim."

"A murderer or a crazed fan?" I asked, not that it really mattered.

"Both."

Then a group of older boys walked past, saw Charlie, and started chanting, "There's only one Charlie Anderson."

Ben and I looked at them like they'd just dropped out of the Welsh skies. But Charlie, well, he was delighted. He high-fived them all and did the running man on the spot. The older kids cheered some more, and even though they were loud I could still hear Ben mumble something about Charlie having no shame.

Anyway, the fact that there were people cheering for Charlie was enough to convince Ben that there might also be the chance of a murderer lurking around, so we scrapped the hitchhiking idea.

I was beginning to wonder if maybe I should have planned things a teeny bit more carefully before we set off from Andover. I think one thing I've learned from the whole experience is that it is a good idea to have a Plan B or even a Plan C ready for when things go wrong and people—in particular, biological fathers—aren't where they're supposed to be. But because I hadn't done any planning about what would happen if we didn't find Alan Froggley at Cardiff Analytics, I had to rely on my cunning and wing it. As group leader it was up to me to come up with a solution, and as group leader I decided we basically had two options.

Option 1: we could use Charlie's winnings to get back to a train station and head home.

Option 2: we could find somewhere to stay in Barry for a night. Get a bus to St. David's early the next morning, find Alan Froggley, and then get back to Andover before anyone missed us.

Thinking about it now, Option 1 does seem like the more sensible thing to do. But at the time it also felt a lot like quitting. Option 2, however, did not feel like quitting. It felt like a very reasonable suggestion. So I didn't mention the first idea and said, "As far as I can see, we only have one option. What do you think about staying here tonight?"

Opinion was divided.

Ben said, "I'm okay with that. I'm not fussed about going home yet."

Charlie's eyes bugged out of his head and he said, "Stay here?"

"It's just for one night."

"But where are we going to sleep?"

It was a good question, but I hadn't quite figured out that part of the plan yet so I said, "We'll find somewhere."

"Somewhere? Does somewhere come with a hypoallergenic pillow?"

"Maybe." I suspected probably not but thought it best not to hit him with a hard no. "It's only for one night."

Ben put his arm around Charlie. "Come on, dude, it will be an adventure. Before you're sent away to Vegans R Us."

"I'm not at all sure about this," Charlie said.

"And you're sure about avocado-and-wheatgrass smoothies? Look, Charlie, in September we're going to be in seventh year in a new school. We might not even be in the same classes. Wouldn't it be cool to have this one last adventure together?" Ben said.

"I guess it would, but so would sleeping in an environment that doesn't trigger my allergies."

"Don't you see, Charlie? This is for Fred. His mom's dead, his Grams is dead. His dad only has one working leg. He's got this weird crinkly haircut . . ." Ben lowered his voice when he mentioned my hair like it was the worst thing of all. "We have to do this. Charlie, tonight you ate a whole raw onion in one minute thirty-seven seconds. That's the fourteenth fastest time the people of Barry have ever witnessed. You, Charlie, are fearless."

Charlie blushed and said, "Ah, it was nothing."

"It wasn't nothing. You were magnificent, Charlie. To the people of Barry, you were a hero. To us, you were a hero. And heroes don't quit."

"You think I was a hero?"

"Absolutely," Ben said. "The way you demolished that onion . . . I'll never forget it. You are a true hero."

By this point I'd been swept along with Ben's motivational talk, so I said, "You're not only a hero, you're one of the best friends a guy could have." Which is true. Not everyone has a mate who'll eat a whole raw onion for them. And I had two.

"You're a winner, Charlie." Ben grabbed us both around the shoulders and shouted, "We're all winners!"

"You guys!" Charlie grinned. "I'm in."

Ben gave me a wink. His own special blend of emotional blackmail and flattery had done the trick.

Now that Charlie was on board I decided we probably needed to get practical about things. "Where can we stay that won't cost us anything?"

It was a puzzling question and we all fell quiet for a moment. Then Ben said, "Guys, I've had an idea."

He really was on a roll and, as ideas go, I thought it wasn't a bad one. Even if it was just a tiny bit illegal.

Looking back now though, I guess it was the start of all the chaos. But we didn't know that at the time.

11

Where we find *Llywelyn-the-Great* and have a humongous fight

Ben rubbed his hands together and said, "Which one do you prefer?" like they all belonged to him.

Charlie thought about it for a while and said, "I like Mavis."

I frowned. "Really? She looks pretty old."

"Some see old, I see charm and elegance."

"I think I prefer Diamond. She's a stunner."

Ben wasn't sure though. "I dunno. Don't you think she's too flashy? Might attract too much attention. I was thinking more along the lines of Ll-y-wel-yn-the-Great. Is that how you pronounce it? Not too big, tucked out of the way, and in the darkest part of the dock."

Ben made a good case and as it was his idea for us to become stowaways for the night, it was only right that he got to pick the boat.

"Llywelyn-the-Great it is," I said, and Ben looked very pleased. Charlie, however, had begun to have doubts.

"Look," Ben said, "we're not doing anything really wrong. Llywelyn is just bobbing about doing nothing. We're only going to sleep on it. We're not going to sail it or anything like that."

"Yeah, what's the worst that could happen?" I said—which I now know was a really dumb thing to say.

We walked up and down the dock a few times, trying not to look suspicious as we scoped out the best way to get onto *Llywelyn-the-Great*. Everyone in Barry was at some pub for a big karaoke event, so luckily there was no one else around.

There wasn't a gangplank onto *Llywelyn* but we reckoned we would be able to make the jump to the ladder. We decided to wait for it to get dark so we could slip aboard unnoticed.

But we got bored of waiting because it was the middle of the summer and it didn't get dark until about ten o'clock. Ben suggested a trip to the Barry amusement arcade to pass the time. He said he was feeling lucky. And when the son of a lottery scratch-card winner says he's feeling lucky, you pay attention.

Ben changed five pounds into 250 two-pence pieces and then over the course of an hour we fed them into the 2p machines and turned them into 625 two-pence pieces!

We felt like kings. I wondered why I hadn't gambled more before. It was easy money.

In hindsight, we should have stopped there, but we didn't. We had the starry eyes and pounding hearts of a slot-machine buzz.

Ben said, "Let's move up to the 10p slots. We could make enough money to pay for a hotel with hypoallergenic pillows," and Charlie and I cheered.

It seemed like a foolproof plan. We changed our winnings into 125 shiny ten-pence pieces—and then very quickly we turned them into just two. I couldn't believe it. We'd spent a fiver and got twenty pence back. It was completely sickening, to be honest. For the first time in my life I understood that saying: *how quickly the mighty have fallen.*

I vowed I'd never gamble again.

Ben, however, had other ideas. He had this crazed look in his eyes and he kept saying that if he could change another fiver he would win the money back and more. Charlie and I weren't having any of it.

Charlie pulled rank and said, "I ate a whole onion for that cash."

Ben couldn't really argue with that, but that didn't stop him from sulking when we left. I think he might have an addictive personality. He should probably look into that.

While Ben moaned about how we'd left before "the big

payout," we tiptoed along the docks toward *Llywelyn-the-Great*. Luckily there still wasn't a soul around. While it was exciting—I was in a foreign land, on an adventure, with my friends—for some reason I couldn't get Dad out of my head. I was worried about how he was doing at home without me to fetch things for him.

I wasn't able to worry about Dad for long though, because soon we were standing opposite our lodgings for the night and the gap between the land and the ladder suddenly seemed a much bigger thing to worry about.

"Has it moved?" Charlie asked. "I'm never going to make that."

"You'll make it," I said, but I wasn't convinced. No offense to Charlie, but he's not exactly aerodynamic.

What he is, however, is powerful and after a short sprint he made the jump easily. As fifth-year long-jump champion, Ben also had no problem covering the distance.

I, on the other hand, sort of messed it up at the last second. I'd opted for a long sprint to maximize my speed. And my sprint was good. I just didn't do the important part at the end and actually jump. So I ended up with my feet still on the dock, my hands clinging to the ladder, the sea lapping below, and Ben and Charlie laughing at me.

Ben crouched down so he was level with my eyeballs. "You alright there, mate?"

"Yeah, great, thanks. Now pull me up before someone sees."

They pulled me up and dropped me on the deck like they'd landed an oversized flounder.

When I was upright again, I had a look around. Truly, *Llywelyn-the-Great* lived up to the "great" part of her name. My experience of boats was limited to one time in a pedal boat at Paulton's Park, a two-man kayak on our camping trip, and the Red Funnel ferry to the Isle of Wight. *Llywelyn* was completely awesome in comparison. Around the edges were cushioned white leather seats and inside the little cabin was a huge steering wheel made of some very shiny wood.

"This is plush," Ben said and stretched out on one of the benches.

It was plush. We'd managed to get aboard a really nice boat without being caught. We were winners again and things were looking like they might work out.

And they probably would have if it wasn't for our humongous fight and what happened because of it.

"I can't believe we're doing this," Charlie said. "My mom would kill me if she knew."

"Don't reckon my dad would even care. He's too busy with Becky to worry about what I'm doing."

"Can you blame him? Becky is lovely. Can't see why you've got such a massive problem with her."

You've probably worked out that Ben is quite sensitive when it comes to Becky. Well, he did not like what Charlie said, so he said, "Right now my *massive* problem is you." Which was a bit harsh.

This got Charlie's back up, so he put on a whiny-fake-Ben voice and said, *"Right now my massive problem is you."*

Ben said, "You're an idiot, Charlie."

Charlie pretended to cry and said, "You said I was a hero."

"You can be both."

"Shut up, Ben."

"Shut up, Charlie."

"Shut up . . ."

They went on for a while telling each other to shut up. They were getting too loud and I was worried that someone might hear, so I said, "Both of you shut up before we end up getting arrested."

That seemed to do the trick.

But then Ben said, "Someone should arrest Charlie for his horrible breath," and they were at each other again.

I shouted, really loudly, "Will you two quit yelling?" I may also have stamped my foot for extra effect.

Thankfully, that did shut them up.

But then Charlie said, "Alright, Fred, chill your beans."

And Ben said, "Yeah, Fred, no need to shout. What's your problem?"

Which was massively annoying as *they* were my problem, but I didn't say anything in case I set them off again. In fact, no one said anything for a while. We just stood there and tried to calm down. I concentrated on the rise and fall of the deck under my feet, wondering whether I should have brought them on my quest to find Alan Froggley. And whether even *I* should have come on this whole stupid journey.

Then Ben said, "Stars are nice tonight." Which I think was code for *I'm sorry for being a jerk.*

And Charlie said, "Sky doesn't look like this back in Andover." Which I think was code for *I'm equally sorry for being a jerk.*

I looked upward. The stars did look especially twinkly. I said, "Do you know we are actually made of stardust? Practically all the elements found on Earth were made in the heart of a star!" Which was not only a really cool fact but also my code for *I forgive you both for being total jerks.*

"Stardust? I like that," Charlie said.

Ben said, "I've never seen so many stars. Look at that one!"

"That's not a star, that's Jupiter," I told him.

"How can you tell?"

"See how it's brighter and more disk-shaped."

"Oh yeah."

"You know, it's mainly made of gas."

Ben said, "A little bit like Charlie then." Which made us laugh. He wasn't wrong. Charlie had been releasing some seriously deadly onion farts.

"You can laugh now," Charlie said. "But you won't be laughing tonight when I fart on your faces while you're asleep."

That shut us up.

"You think we might see a shooting star if we look hard enough?" I asked.

"If we do, what would you wish for?"

It was too big a question to answer, so I said, "For Charlie to stop farting. That or peace on Earth."

"I'd wish for better friends," Charlie said and thumped me on the leg, which I guess I deserved. Then he said, "Actually, I'd wish for my mom to stop going on about broccoli and let me indulge in my carnivorous urges."

Ben didn't seem to like that idea, as he said, "Out of all the things in the world, *that's* what you'd wish for?"

"You remember in third year when some kids got a letter home after we were weighed and measured by the school nurse?"

Ben and I both nodded.

"Well, I got a letter home. And it's no coincidence that

after that Mom put the whole family on her ridiculous "Anderson Healthy Lifestyle Change" and she started buying avocadoes and quinoa in bulk. She thinks I'm too fat."

"You're not too fat," I said. "Just...you know...sturdy."

"You think? Sturdy...sturdy..." Charlie tried the word out. "Yeah, I like that. Makes me sound solid."

"Another very good description," I said.

He swiveled around to face Ben. "You know what? You're right. That wasn't a great wish. What I really wish is that Mom would realize that I'm happy as I am."

Ben nodded. "Now that's an alright kind of wish."

Nobody said anything for a while.

Then Ben spoke so quietly that I could barely hear him, but I caught what he said. He said, "I'd wish for Becky to disappear and for my mom and dad to get back together."

"Would that make you happy?" I asked.

"Yeah, it would."

"Didn't your parents argue all the time?" It was an innocent question, but it did not go over well.

Ben's face got all twisted like when he was eating his onion.

"Shut up, Fred. You don't know anything about my parents."

I probably should have left it, but I didn't.

"Don't tell me to shut up. You shut up."

"You shut up."

"No, *you* shut up."

We were back to the whole telling-each-other-to-shut-up. Again.

Eventually Ben really lost it. He stood up so that he was looking down at me and shouted, "I'll tell you to shut up if I want to! You think you know everything—ranting on about your facts all the time. Like anybody cares that onions and garlic are cousins."

That was too much. People love my facts. I got to my feet and stared him right in the eyes. "Don't get mad at me because your parents hate each other."

Even at the time I knew I shouldn't have said that, but I couldn't help myself. It had been a long day and I think I was tired and overly emotional. I guess he was feeling the same, because things quickly got even more out of hand.

Ben stared right back at me. "You think you know everything. But you're stupid—just like your dad."

I know! He went there.

And then he went there again. "Oh sorry, I forgot. He's not your dad, is he?"

That's when *I* lost it.

I grabbed him and said, "Say that again."

Ben laughed and said, "Or what?"

I didn't actually have an answer, and luckily Charlie pushed himself between us. "Guys, maybe you should calm down. I've got a packet of Skittles we could share—"

Ben didn't break eye contact with me as he said, "Butt out, Charlie." He knocked the Skittles out of Charlie's hand and they spilled across the deck.

Charlie did not take too kindly to losing his little taste of the rainbow—he pushed us both and said, "Do not tell me to butt out."

"This has nothing to do with you," I said, which seemed to really annoy Charlie.

"That's typical. Think you can laugh at me and leave me out like always." He apparently had his own issues he wanted to settle.

"You want to get involved in a fight?" Ben said.

"Yeah, I do."

"Fine."

"We're doing this then, fighting?" I asked. To be one hundred percent honest, I was already beginning to have second thoughts.

Ben poked me in the chest unnecessarily hard. "Yeah, we are."

I grabbed his T-shirt and said, "Okay then. Prepare to die," because I thought it sounded threatening.

Charlie wrapped his arms around both of us so tight that we were like a twelve-limbed body with three heads.

I didn't know what to do next. I'd never been in a fight before and I knew Charlie and Ben hadn't either. So we held on to each other's T-shirts and kind of pulled and shoved. I don't know if anyone threw any punches— I suspect not. All we did was stagger from one side of the boat to the other. Until the inevitable happened and we fell in.

12

Charlie Anderson should never be left to do laundry

It's amazing what an unexpected dip in the sea can do to break the tension. Once we had hauled ourselves back onto *Llywelyn-the-Great* and had caught our breath, all the anger seemed to have drained out of us into the Welsh water.

"That was unexpected," I said.

"My phone's dead," Ben said, trying to turn it off and back on again.

I pulled mine out of my sopping pocket. "Mine too."

Charlie peered over the side. "Think mine's still in the sea."

"What were we doing?" I said. "That was so stupid."

"I dunno. I felt like I really wanted to fight you." Ben shook his head to get the water out of his ears.

"Yeah, I thought I wanted to fight you too," I said.

Ben stopped shaking and looked at me. "I don't really want to fight you."

"I don't really want to fight you either. Friends?"

"Friends."

It was a nice moment but it was cut short when Charlie stood between us and shook himself like a dog. "I don't mind what you guys are doing as long as you don't leave me out."

"We promise not to leave you out," I said.

"Good. Or I'll get you both." He took his shirt off, wrung it out, and whipped me and then Ben around the legs. He chased us around the boat until we got tired and then we all flopped down on the padded benches.

"What are we going to do now?" Ben asked. "I'm cold. Are you cold?"

I nodded. "I don't want to stay out here all night."

"We should go below deck. Keep warm in the cabin."

"It's probably locked," I said.

Charlie tried the handle. "It's definitely locked."

"It's probably not *locked* locked though." Before we could stop him, Ben gave the handle a shake, then rammed into the door with his shoulder. There was a splintering sound and the door swung open. "See, not *locked* locked."

"I can't believe you just did that," Charlie said.

"We're already trespassing, I didn't think a little

breaking and entering was much different," Ben said, switching on the light. "We are in a moment of extreme need."

I looked at Charlie and he sighed and said, "Do you think they have hypoallergenic pillows in prison?"

Despite the threat of a criminal record hovering over our heads, I couldn't help but feel relieved that we were inside. We started exploring, leaving wet footprints wherever we went. At one end of the boat was a small kitchen area, in the middle section was a tiny table with some seats, and at the other end was the world's smallest toilet and bunks for sleeping. I told Ben and Charlie not to touch anything. We had to leave everything exactly how we'd found it.

I was so tired, and Ben and Charlie were yawning too, so I suggested we strip off and put on our spare underpants to get ready for bed. We needed to be up early and out of the boat before anyone else was about.

Charlie took our wet clothes—he said he'd found somewhere to dry them out—and then we climbed into the bunks. Ben and I went top-and-tail on the bottom bunk. Charlie had the top one to himself. We should have gone the other way around because Charlie kept farting, but by that point I couldn't be bothered to move. It wasn't long before we passed out, either from fatigue or from the toxic fumes of Charlie's onion-scented butt blasts.

It must have been only a few hours later that I was woken up by a shrill wailing sound. I bolted up, my nose twitching.

Smoke.

It took me a moment to remember where I was and then work out that the boat must be on fire. I shook Charlie and Ben awake.

"Get up. I think the boat is on fire!"

Charlie stretched, rubbed his eyes, and then appeared to remember something and leaped to his feet. "Oh no! I forgot!"

I did NOT like the sound of that. "What did you forget, Charlie?"

He didn't answer, just ran off in his underpants toward the other end of the boat. Ben and I followed him to the little kitchen area. He opened the sliding door and all this smoke billowed out.

He picked up a kitchen towel and waved it around while saying, "No, no, no, no, no," like a severely disappointed folk dancer.

"What did you do?" Ben shouted.

"Have you been cooking?" Through the smoke I could make out a pile of something ablaze on the stove top.

I filled up a mug with water from the sink and threw it at the pile. To be honest, it had as much effect as peeing into a volcano. Luckily, Ben grabbed the little fire extinguisher that was attached to the wall, pulled the nozzle, and aimed it at the stove. The small blaze was extinguished, and we spluttered and coughed as even more smoke filled the cabin. The fire alarm was still going so I grabbed the towel from Charlie and tried waving it in front of it. That didn't do anything so I began pushing the off switch, but it wouldn't stop.

Charlie yelled helpfully, "Turn it off. Someone's going to hear us!"

"What do you think I'm trying to do?"

Ben opened the door to let out some of the smoke and I found a wooden spoon in one of the kitchen drawers. I adopted a more aggressive approach and began whacking the alarm with all my strength. It fell from the ceiling onto the floor but the noise got louder if anything.

"Take that!"

WHACK!

"And that!"

WHACK!

"Go on, Fred, smash it!" Charlie yelled.

I really started to pummel the alarm. The white plastic casing cracked, then fell apart, and the alarm emitted its final death wails.

"Finish it off!" Ben shouted.

I brought the spoon down right in the center of the

alarm and delivered the killer blow. It let out a final peep and then was quiet. Freddie Yates 1—Smoke Detector 0.

"Enjoy that much?" Ben asked.

I blushed. I had in an angry-fun sort of way. "Well . . . you know."

"He's got a kitchen utensil and he's not afraid to use it," Charlie laughed.

I poked the smoldering ashes with the spoon. They looked strangely familiar. "What is this stuff?"

Charlie quickly stopped laughing and began shifting his weight from foot to foot in a way that made him look decidedly . . . *shifty.*

"Charlie?"

"I only meant to warm them up. I didn't think they'd catch on fire."

In among the ashes I spotted a charred label with *AGE 11–12 YRS* printed on it. "Charlie, tell me this isn't what I think it is."

"It's our clothes."

"I said not to tell me that."

Charlie looked uncomfortable. "It seemed like a good idea at the time."

"To cook our clothes?" Ben spluttered. "What were you going to do—eat them?"

"There weren't any flames, the stove has these hot circles, see?"

"Hot circles?" I couldn't believe what I was hearing.

"I was only going to warm them through."

"Charlie! They were our clothes, not pancakes. We've got nothing to wear apart from our underpants! I can't meet Alan Froggley in my underpants. I just can't."

It was then that Ben inexplicably started laughing and I had a serious sense-of-humor failure. "Ben, this isn't funny!"

"It's a little funny."

"No, it's a disaster."

"Now you're being dramatic."

"Ben, we're in Wales, in a boat we've broken into, that we've now set on fire, and we're practically naked—how is this not a disaster?"

Ben rolled his eyes. "Chill, nobody's died, have they?"

His words seemed to fill the whole cabin.

He looked at me guiltily. "Oh. Sorry. Apart from your Grams. Nobody else has died."

I just looked at him with my mouth open.

Ben quickly broke eye contact, picked up the bits of alarm, and chucked them in the garbage can. "It's fine. We'll think of something."

I couldn't see how it was fine. "We'll need a miracle to get ourselves out of this mess."

But a miracle didn't happen. Not then anyway. In fact, our situation got a whole lot worse.

13

Charlie, Ben, and I find some
stuff and do a runner

I was eager to get going on our journey, so while Charlie tried unsuccessfully to clean the smoke stains off the kitchen wall with a toothbrush, Ben and I conducted a search of the boat to find some clothes. The little clock on the kitchen stove told us it was coming up on five in the morning. We needed to be gone by six at the latest to make sure nobody was about.

Ben looked through a tiny cupboard at the back of the boat while I started to look through some drawers. It was when I rifled through the bottom drawer that our journey took a serious turn for the unexpected.

I gasped.

Then I blinked.

Then I rubbed my eyes.

I think I might have done one more gasp and then I slammed the drawer shut.

"Everything alright, Fred?" Ben asked finally.

A funny little squeaky sound came out of my mouth. A noise I haven't made before or since.

"You okay? What did you find?"

I couldn't answer. I couldn't think. My brain was trapped on one image. The image of that Fiona Bruce woman with the lovely set of teeth looking utterly dismayed on the *Antiques Roadshow*.

"Fred, you gone mute or something?" Ben opened the drawer to take a look. "Very nice but they're not going to cover much up, are they?"

I managed to squeeze some words out. They were: "Ben, Ben, see? Uh-oh?"

Ben frowned.

Granted, they weren't the most informative words, so I tried again. "Ben, do you know what these are?"

"Er, yeah. I'm not an idiot. They're rings. Ugly ones at that."

It was at this moment that everything got a little crazy. Charlie stumbled into the room doing a weird wobbly scream. His face was white and he was carrying something in his hand. "Guys, guuuuuys! I think you should see this."

My eyes flew open so wide I thought my eyeballs might fall out.

"Good grief, Charlie! Where did you get that?" Ben shouted.

"In the right-hand cupboard under the sink, next to the fabric softener and in front of the dish soap."

He was surprisingly precise given the circumstances.

"What's a gun doing next to the dish soap?" I yelled.

"Put it down! It could be loaded," Ben said.

Charlie placed the gun down on the bottom bunk, took a step back, and started to whimper. His legs buckled very slowly, and he sort of accordianed down onto the floor and began rocking back and forth.

Even though I was wearing practically nothing, I started to feel really hot. Like, volcano-hot. "Guys, we need to get out of here."

"Fred, what's going on?" Ben asked.

I held up two rather ugly but apparently priceless gold swan rings. "My dad was watching something about these on the news."

"Fred, what are you talking about?"

"Guys, I think we may have broken into a boat owned by a jewel thief. A jewel thief who owns a gun!"

The information seemed to hang in the air for a moment before they fully took it in. Then Charlie began rocking faster and Ben ran around in tiny circles muttering unhelpful things like, "Oh my oh my oh my oh my. They're going to kill us. I'm too young to die."

All the rocking and running did not help my own stress levels, and when Ben grabbed hold of my arms and said,

"Fred, what do we do? Think of something," all I could think to say was, "Do you know a male swan is called a cob and a female swan is called a pen and mute swans have a top speed of fifty-five miles an hour?"

Charlie stopped rocking. Then he and Ben looked at me with these bewildered expressions until Ben said, "What the actual hell, Fred?"

"Sorry—I don't know why I said that."

"Well, let's make like a swan and leave, like, now," Ben said.

Charlie pulled himself to his feet and then said, "Hang on—in our underpants?"

"You want to wait for the owner of that gun to come back?"

Charlie shook his head.

"Didn't think so. Come on, let's go."

We fled *Llywelyn-the-Now-Slightly-Less-Great* in our damp shoes and underpants, sprinting out of the broken front door into the gray morning light. I cleared the gap between the boat and the dock the first try. I think the extra injection of fear propelled me across the distance. We pounded along the dock with no clue where we were headed, just as long as we were away from the boat . . . and the gun.

We found ourselves back in the park. Ben stopped first and pulled me and Charlie behind this great big bush that, while providing excellent cover, was super prickly. The park was deserted—the stage was still there, but the booths were closed. People wouldn't be arriving for the festival until around ten o'clock, when the scarecrow competition judging began.

"What are we going to do now?" Charlie asked. "Do you think we should go to the police? Tell them what we've found?"

Ben did not like that idea. "Can you imagine how much trouble we'd be in? We could end up with a criminal record. Or worse."

"Do you mean prison?" I asked.

"I dunno, maybe. We did break and enter and Charlie's also an arsonist, so it's a possibility."

"Okay, so no going to the police, agreed?" I looked at them both and they nodded.

"I think we need to get out of Barry," Ben said.

Ben was absolutely right. I was ready to get as far away from Barry as possible, but there was a problem. "If we get on a bus in only our underwear, people will ask questions."

"We need to find some clothes," Charlie said.

"You think?" Ben snapped a little uncharitably. "Where are we going to get clothes at five in the morning?"

It was a good question.

Sometimes there are good questions that are easy to

answer, like *How many people live on Earth?* (There's around 7.8 billion, by the way.) Sometimes there are good questions that are tricky to answer, like *Which animal would be the cutest if it was shrunk down to the size of a mouse?* (I mean, how do you even start?) And then there are good questions that seem impossible to answer, but the solution sort of jumps out at you from nowhere. And this was that type of good question, because after Ben said, "Where are we going to get clothes at five in the morning?" I said, "From there."

14

We first realize that the
Gaffer might be after us

It took Ben and Charlie a second before they realized that I was pointing at the entries for the scarecrow competition. Ben looked at me, smiled, and then before I had a chance to tell him how it was going to work, he raced off shouting, "Bagsy Batman!"

That wasn't happening—no way was he getting Batman. It was my fantastic solution, so I should get to choose. Ben did not agree with my reasoning—he picked up Batman and ran off with the super-scarecrow under his arm, trailing straw behind him. He wouldn't stop even when he could see I was getting mad. He's a really good runner. I was never going to catch him. So in the end I said, "Fine, you take it if you're going to be so childish."

That left Spiderman and Supergirl.

Supergirl was not an option.

Charlie must have realized that at the same time as me, because he launched himself at the Spiderman scarecrow, yelling, "Spidey's mine!"

I tried everything to get the Spiderman scarecrow out from under Charlie but, on account of his sturdiness, my efforts were futile.

I ended up stuck with Supergirl.

I was furious but, on reflection, Charlie would never have fitted into the Supergirl outfit, so I guess it was a foregone conclusion I'd end up wearing it. I was not going to pretend to be happy about it though.

"Don't look so miserable," Ben said. "It actually really suits you. The skirt sort of flicks out when you walk."

"Shut up." I turned my back to them and the skirt did a pleasing flutter as I spun. I wanted to do another little spin, but I waited until Ben and Charlie weren't watching.

"Are we keeping the masks?" Charlie asked. "I don't feel complete without the mask."

"You bet we're keeping the masks," Ben said, putting his on top of his head.

"Fine," I said with a fake sigh, because there was no way I was leaving mine behind, but they didn't need to know that.

We put the scarecrows back as best as we could. One of them had lost an arm and Supergirl's head was drooping to one side in a way that was not anatomically possible, so I wouldn't say our presentation was of award-winning quality.

I still feel a little guilty about destroying Clementine's hard work. But frankly, we needed something to wear more than the scarecrows did.

Unfortunately, superhero costumes do not come with pockets, which is a massive oversight. Everybody needs pockets, even superheroes. But fortunately, the material is super clingy, which meant that when we put our money into our underpants it felt like it was being held in quite securely.

Before we left the park, there was one thing I had to do. I pulled the two gold swan rings out of my underpants and stuffed them onto one scarecrow's hand.

Ben looked at me, wide-eyed. "You took those?"

"I did. But by mistake. I kind of panicked. What with the gun and all . . ."

"You stole priceless rings from a thief with a gun? Do you have a death wish?"

"I told you, I wasn't thinking. The thief won't know it was me who took them. If we just leave them here, maybe they'll be handed in to the police."

Charlie looked confused. "Dude, that's a scarecrow, it's not going to hand anything in."

"I figured Big Trev and his mom would hand them

in. See, I think there's a reward. If it's fifty pounds, that would make up for Ben getting Big Trev disqualified yesterday. Guys, we have totally ruined the whole Barry Festival for them."

"I wouldn't say I got him disqualified as such."

I gave him a look that said, *You're not kidding anybody.*

"Are we sure leaving the rings here is a good idea?" Charlie asked.

"We can't exactly take them to a police station ourselves, can we? We'd have to tell them about how we found them and that would mean confessing to breaking and entering. And then I could forget about going off to find Alan Froggley."

"Alright," Ben said. "Let's just leave them and go."

We left the three sorry-looking scarecrows and headed into the center of Barry. As none of us had working phones, we had to find out the old-fashioned way what time the buses went, by checking the schedule at the bus stop. We'd done timetables in fifth year so we were well prepared. However, we were not prepared for the fact that there was no direct bus route from Barry to St. David's.

"What now?" Charlie gave me a look like our situation was all *my* fault, which was incredible as he was the one who cooked our clothes.

I slid off the narrow bus-stop bench for the umpteenth

time. Lycra and smooth surfaces = zero traction. "I guess we keep heading west. The first bus is in twenty minutes and it's headed to Gileston. The timetable reckons it's a thirty-two-minute trip."

Ben kicked an empty Coke can in my direction. "Wow. What a plan." His tone wasn't helping the situation in the slightest.

"What's your plan then?"

I think I wobbled my head in a slightly patronizing way because he wobbled his head back at me and said, "What about a taxi?"

I hadn't thought about a taxi. I couldn't deny it, it wasn't a bad idea.

Charlie must have thought so too because he said, "Good plan, Batman."

Ben gave me this scrunchy-faced smile and said, "And that's why I got to wear the cool costume."

He led the way to the taxi stand with this smug little swagger. I waited until he was a few feet in front and then stuck my tongue out at him behind his back. I only did it once though. Okay, twice.

There was only one cab at the stand. It was silver and had *BIG T'S CABS* written in black across the hood. Ben and Charlie suddenly got shy and pushed me forward to speak to the hairy man sitting in the driver's seat. I peered in through the window. He had a full-sleeve tattoo that included a picture of the Welsh flag, a dragon, and a detailed map of Wales, which must have been very useful for a taxi driver.

I cleared my throat. "Excuse me, sir. How much for a taxi to St. David's?"

He looked me up and down and said, "One hundred and fifty quid, but for you, princess, I'll make it one forty-five."

While I was flattered that my Supergirl outfit had got us a five-pound discount, we had nowhere near that kind of cash.

"Guess we're bussing it," Charlie sighed.

As we turned to leave, the cab's radio buzzed.

"Go ahead, Dave, what you got for me?" the hairy man said into it.

"Stu, the Gaffer wants all drivers to keep a lookout for three boys seen running from his boat in the early hours of this morning."

My stomach lurched and I almost vomited through the taxi window. It was very obvious that we were three boys. Charlie, Ben, and I exchanged worried glances.

Stu pressed his radio button. "Any description?"

We quickly pulled our masks down to cover our faces after he said that.

"Er, yeah. They're only wearing their underpants. One of them is a bit overweight."

I gulped and tried not to look at Charlie, who was doing his best to suck his stomach in, but Lycra is an unforgiving material to wear.

"Reckons they're between the ages of eight and sixteen."

Eight? Eight! I wasn't sure who he thought was eight! In hindsight I think he was probably talking about Ben. He does have an immature way about him sometimes.

"What they gone and done?" Stu asked as he picked his teeth.

"Dunno. But the Gaffer is pretty anxious to find 'em. He don't sound happy."

"Okay, Dave. I'll keep 'em peeled. Got three kids with me at the moment. But they've definitely got clothes on and one's a girl."

I didn't know whether to be insulted or relieved.

When Stu put his receiver away, I said, "Thank you for your time," in my best girl-like voice. Then we ran as fast as we could to the bus stop.

As we rounded the corner we saw that the 303 bus to Gileston was signaling to pull away from the bus stop. Ben raced ahead and managed to bang on the window. The driver let us on but he seemed grumpy about it, even though we were his only passengers.

"Guys, what's a gaffer?" Charlie panted as we made

our way down the bus aisle. "Is it something to do with that sticky-tape stuff?"

Ben said, "A gaffer is another word for a boss, you doughnut."

"Oh, that makes more sense. Do you think the gaffer they were talking about owned the boat? Do you reckon he knows we stole his stolen goods?"

I flopped down on the back seat and Ben and Charlie sat on either side of me. "I dunno . . . yes, maybe. But I'm glad we're not sticking around to find out."

"I thought we were done for back there. Lucky Fred's got such a pretty face," Ben said, squishing my cheeks.

"Get off." I batted him away. I wasn't in the mood. "This morning has been a total nightmare."

"It hasn't been great," Ben agreed.

Charlie pulled his Spiderman mask back up so that it sat on top of his head. "You don't think he'll come after us—the Gaffer?" His face had gone the same greenish-white color it went before he threw up after a ride on the Tilt-a-Whirl at the Andover fair.

"Nah, there's no way he'll know it was us," I said, but my brain had started whirling.

Charlie's face changed back to its normal pinkish color. "Yeah, you're right. Hey, anyone want a peanut?" He magically produced a bag of peanuts from somewhere inside his costume.

I tipped my head back and closed my eyes. I didn't want peanuts. I just wanted quiet for a bit. I needed to think. "That was more than enough excitement for one day."

"You sound like my grandma," Charlie laughed. And then his face fell. "Ah, sorry, Fred. Forgot your Grams is dead."

"That's okay."

"Hey, Fred."

"Yes, Charlie?"

"Do you reckon there's a Giles finally resting in Gileston?"

"Charlie, do you think we could have some shush?"

"Okay, Fred."

I settled back into my seat and closed my eyes. To start with, I enjoyed the little bit of peace and quiet, but then I began to go over the events of the morning in my mind. And then I began to quietly freak out.

I couldn't shake the feeling that there was a chance the Gaffer would figure out that it was us who'd been on *Llywelyn-the-Great*, broken a door, started a fire, ruined his toothbrush, and stolen his rings. We'd probably left fingerprints all over the place.

The smart thing to do would have been to give up and go home. But when I thought about going back without ever meeting my biological father, especially after everything we'd been through to get here, I got this horrible aching feeling in my belly.

I realize now that the aching feeling was more about Grams. I guess when you're lost in a strange place it's not so easy to figure things out. At the time, though, my mind was set on one thing—finishing my journey to find Alan Froggley. For that to happen, we'd have to be way more careful and keep a low profile. That meant no more breaking and entering, no more accidental arson, and no more robbery.

But keeping a low profile turned out to be much harder than I had anticipated.

15

This is where we meet Albert and Phyllis Griffiths. Oh, and PC Mike

The thirty-two-minute bus ride was uneventful, apart from one near-choking incident where Ben threw a peanut into Charlie's mouth with such force that Charlie claimed it had bruised his epiglottis. After Ben had finished examining the inside of Charlie's throat and Charlie had stopped going on and on about his ruptured epiglottal tissue, I told them that from then on, we had to go about our business in a less conspicuous way.

"Absolutely on board with that," Charlie said. And then he said, "What's conspicuous mean?"

I explained, "We have to blend into the shadows. If we see trouble, we run in the other direction."

Charlie nodded then spit into his hand and held it out. I do not really agree with spit promises because it has been estimated that there are over one hundred million bacteria microbes in every millimeter of saliva, but our situation was serious, so I spat into my hand and Ben did the same. We pressed them together and I tried not to think about the three-hundred-million-bacteria-jungle oozing between my fingers. The whole thing was disgusting but I felt calmer that they were on board.

Unfortunately, the calm feeling did not last for long and our spit promise to remain shadowlike was broken before the saliva had even dried on our palms. And for that I blame Phyllis and Albert . . . oh, and PC Mike—he should shoulder some of the responsibility too.

We stepped off the bus into what I now know is one of the tiniest villages in South Wales. I remember thinking, *Brilliant, we can't get into any trouble here.* All we had to do was hang around until there was another bus going in the direction we needed.

The first person we saw in Gileston was this sweet little old lady singing "All Things Bright and Beautiful" at the top of her lungs. She was hobbling up the road toward us, wearing a knitted green hat with a red pom-pom and swinging her purse.

She seemed so loud, so alive. I only stopped watching her when Charlie nudged me and said, "Hey, Fred, what's he up to?"

He was pointing at an old man who was crouching down behind a stone wall. There was something about him that made him look suspicious. I don't know whether it was the steely look in his gray eyes or his big wispy eyebrows. Perhaps it was the shovel that he was gripping tightly in his leathery tanned hands while he hid.

I said, "I don't know, Charlie," because I didn't know.

"Well, he doesn't look like he's about to do any gardening," Ben said.

The old man popped his head over the wall, spotted the little old lady, and then ducked back down. The little old lady continued to make her way along the road, praising the Lord for all creatures great and small at full volume.

The old man popped his head up again, sized up the old woman, and ducked back down like he did before. His lips were moving, as though he was speaking to himself. He gripped the shovel tighter. All in all, it was very curious behavior.

"You know what?" Ben said. "I think he's going to hit that old woman with that shovel."

I had to agree. It certainly looked like that.

"What are we going to do about it?" Ben asked. "We can't stand here and watch that happen."

I'm ashamed to say that a teeny part of me was worried that running down the street dressed as superheroes was hardly keeping a low profile. But the bigger, less awful part of me could not stand by and watch an old lady being pummeled with a shovel. So I pulled down my mask, flipped my cape behind me, and raced off down the path toward her. I have to admit I did feel a little awesome to be charging to help someone with my cape flapping behind me.

As the old lady belted out the final words, "The Lord God made them all," the old man leaped out from behind the wall and shouted, "Shame on you, Phyllis Griffiths!" and held his shovel above his head.

He didn't do this for long though, because Charlie, Ben, and I charged in and rugby-tackled him below the knees. He landed on the pavement with an "Oomph!" It was pretty cool.

Phyllis Griffiths shrieked. The old man yelled. We clung onto his legs as hard as we could while he flopped around like a geriatric octopus in a tweed cap.

"Don't worry, Missus Old Lady," Ben said. "We've got him."

"B-B-Batman?" the old woman stuttered.

Because the angry man with the shovel was safely pinned under Charlie's butt, Ben let go and offered a gloved hand. "At your service."

The old woman slowly shook Ben's hand. Her forehead had gone extra wrinkly. "Who are you people? Are you . . . ? You can't be . . . ?"

Before I could respond, Ben said, "We're here to help, ma'am," like he was a proper superhero!

The old man who was still squashed underneath Charlie and I groaned. "Will you get off, immediately? He's not Batman, Phyllis, he's just a kid."

"I may be just a kid." Ben lifted up his mask. "But I'm a kid who fights for good."

Frankly, he'd got completely carried away with the whole superhero thing by this point.

The old man spat out an angry laugh. "Good? She's rotten to her core."

Phyllis rolled her eyes. "Oh, quiet down, Albert. You're making a spectacle of yourself."

This was an interesting turn of events. "You know this man?" I asked.

Phyllis Griffiths looked me up and down. "Yes, Wonder Woman, I do."

"It's Supergirl," I corrected her and then regretted it because Ben smirked and said, "See, I knew you'd find it easy to get into character."

I ignored him and turned back to Phyllis. "How do you know this man?"

"He's my brother."

"Your brother? He was about to hit you with a shovel!"

Albert squirmed beneath us. "I wasn't going to hit her with a shovel."

I squashed him down harder. "It *looked* like you were going to hit her with a shovel. You can't go around hitting old women with shovels, even if you are related to them."

"I wasn't going to hit her, I was going to threaten her with it. Now would you two get off me!"

I thought about this for a moment but decided that threatening someone with a shovel probably still constituted a criminal offense, so I pressed on with my interrogation. "Why were you threatening her?"

"Because it's all her fault they've gone. I told you not to go showing 'em off but you didn't listen, did you? Mother left them to both of us."

Phyllis Griffiths rummaged through her purse, pulled out a small potato like it was a totally normal thing to carry around, and threw it at Albert. "This again, Albert?" The potato just missed his head and landed on the pavement.

"It's because of you that they've gone and now you need to pay me for my share! Give me what you owe me," Albert snarled.

"I'll give you a good beating." This time she produced a pear from her bag and threw it in Albert's direction, but she missed, and it hit a rather muscular but weirdly young-looking policeman who had appeared from around the corner.

"What's with all the produce grenades? Can someone

explain to me what's occurring here?" He didn't sound happy.

Charlie puffed his chest up. "Officer, we have reprimanded this man who we believe to be called Albert."

Ben stepped forward. "Because he was about to hit—"

"Threaten," Albert interrupted.

Ben continued, "Okay, *threaten* this lady with a shovel. And we have sworn a promise that whenever you're in trouble . . . we'll be there on the double."

I snorted when he said that. *That* line was from the *Paw Patrol* theme song. Ben had got his superhero oaths mixed up.

The policeman folded his thick arms across his chest, looked heavenward, and muttered something about giving him strength. He had a few wisps of hair on his chin that twinkled in the sunlight. They reminded me of Grams, which made me do a long sigh. I missed her whiskery face.

The cop turned his attention back to Phyllis. "Is this true, Phyllis?"

"Yes, he was going to bludgeon me with that there shovel."

"I already said I wasn't going to attack you, I was going to threaten you—scare you a little."

"Pah! Scare me? Never," Phyllis chuckled, and I believed her. Up close, she had that determined-old-lady look. Grams had it sometimes. Like when she caught me hiding broccoli in my pockets instead of eating it, or when Dad tried to wear a tracksuit to Mr. Burnley's retirement party. And when I was in third year and she stormed into school because I'd got myself in a state about not having a mother to write a poem about for the Mother's Day assembly. I'd give anything to see her with that look in her eye again.

The policeman rolled his shoulders back and said, "Right. Let's get the situation under control."

That seemed like a good idea. I didn't have time to be hanging around sitting on old people, I had Alan Froggley to find.

The policeman produced a phone from his pocket. "Can I take a photo?"

"For evidence?" I asked.

"No, for the Gileston newspaper. My other job is being the village journalist. Three kids preventing an attack is the biggest story we've had here for . . . well forever really."

This did not seem very professional to me. "Isn't that a conflict of interest—to be a policeman and a reporter?"

"It's never been a problem before. Go on, girlie. One photo, please?"

I did not want people seeing a photo of me in a Supergirl outfit. Even if it was for a local paper with a readership of about twelve. So I said, "No photo."

"Aw, go on, don't be shy. You'd be doing me a massive favor."

"I'm fine with it," Ben said.

I shot him my *You'd better not be fine with it* look, but he either didn't realize or chose to ignore it, because he said, "Where's the best lighting?"

Charlie had already adopted his insta-pout, so I knew I wouldn't be getting any backup from him.

"This is hardly keeping a low profile," I hissed.

Ben snapped the back of my outfit. "Don't get your leotard in a twist. No one's going to know it's us. Go on, it will be a laugh."

They weren't going to give in, so I told the policeman-journalist-man, "Fine, but we want to remain anonymous." I also made Ben and Charlie pull their masks down as a precaution. While they adopted various power poses for the photo, I halfheartedly swished my skirt and told myself it was extremely unlikely that Gileston news would spread far. Still, there was an angry Gaffer out there who might be looking for us and potentially even angrier parents back in Andover. But I pushed all that out of my mind because I needed to focus on my journey to find the parent I thought I was desperate to meet.

16

Hooray! We score some transport! Of sorts

After the photo, PC Mike—that was the policeman-journalist—let Albert off with a stern warning and a reminder that he still had thirty hours of community service outstanding. This was for the time he put a goat in Phyllis's garden and it ate Gileston's prize-winning roses. Albert had a reputation as a troublemaker. His war against his sister had begun a few weeks earlier following an argument over some family heirlooms and he could not let the matter drop.

A little more questioning by any one of us at this point would have revealed that we had information about the very heirlooms in question. But we didn't ask, so we didn't make the connection until much later, after the seagull had died. (You'll understand when we get to it.)

Mike confiscated Albert's shovel and Albert trudged back to his house, muttering angrily to himself about how

Mike was a crooked cop. Mike got upset about this, but when Phyllis said, "You're a big brave policeman now, Michael. Rise above it," he managed to pull himself together.

As a reward for our heroics, Phyllis invited us back for tea and cake. We had a quick group meeting to decide whether this was a good idea—after all, Phyllis *was* a stranger. But as we were all hungry and a policeman slash journalist was there, we did not see any sense in turning down free food. Although we might have if she'd told us what was on offer sooner. Pear-and-potato turnovers take some getting used to.

Her house was a little stone cottage less than a minute around the corner. While Phyllis busied herself in the kitchen, Mike sat down at the kitchen table, looking right at home—which we later found out was because he was. He double-clicked his pen, clearly very excited to write his newspaper article.

"Tell me, what brings you to Gileston?"

I immediately felt uncomfortable. I'd crack under the pressure of a police interrogation. I'd spill everything—that we were runaways, trespassers, thieves, and arsonists. We'd be sent away to a facility to be corrected and I'd never get to meet Alan Froggley. No—it would be best to say nothing. I tried my *Keep your mouths shut* look on Ben and Charlie.

Incredibly, Charlie did not pick up on my look.

He frowned at me and then started to speak. "We're looking—" I elbowed him in the side and a chunk of potato or pear—it was hard to tell which—fell out of his mouth.

Ben must have picked up on my look because he said, "We're on vacation with Fred's family."

"As in Frederica? How are you spelling that?"

"As in Fred. F R E D."

Mike looked at me, then did a double take. "Sorry, mate. I thought you were a girl. What with your skirt and all."

I sighed. The whole girl thing was getting a little annoying. Although Charlie and Ben thought it was hilarious. I had finished off an entire pear-and-potato turnover before they stopped laughing at me.

"So, can you give me your full names?" Mike's pen hovered over his notepad.

"Charlie—Ow!"

I'd kicked Charlie under the table.

I said, "We'd like to remain anonymous."

Mike nodded but I saw him write down *Charlie Ow* on his notepad. What a doofus.

He wasn't looking too inspired. "You're not giving me much, guys."

Phyllis set a pot of tea down in the middle of the table and ruffled his hair. "Don't worry, you'll come up with something folks will want to read. You'll find your angle."

Mike puffed out his cheeks. "I hope you're not

suggesting I fabricate a piece of journalism? Absolutely not. I would rather die than compromise my professional integrity."

It is hard to believe those words came out of his mouth now, considering what he did put in print. PC Mike found an angle all right. And it was a full 180 degrees away from the truth.

Phyllis offered some beet-and-raspberry scones and put one on my plate even though I'd said in my clearest voice, "No thank you very much, beet is not my favorite." Which is how Grams taught me to politely turn down food I don't want to eat.

Phyllis spread a thick layer of Marmite across her scone, dipped it in her tea, and then stared at me with her milky blue eyes, which made me think of Grams again. (Her eyes—not the Marmite scone.)

"Where's your family then?"

It felt like a big question, so I said, "Do you know Marmite is made from brewer's yeast and was discovered by accident?"

Phyllis raised an eyebrow. "Well, isn't that a small miracle?"

The discovery of Marmite is not a small miracle, but I let it go because I thought I had distracted her from asking me about my family.

"So why are you boys in Gileston on your own?"

A lump of beet scone got stuck in my throat. I've always been a horrible liar. Luckily Ben is excellent at it. He flashed Phyllis a big smile. "As I said, we're on vacation and we thought we'd check out the local area."

"I see. Where are you staying?"

My heart was hammering in my chest, but I couldn't detect any trace of stress on Ben's face when he said, "Little village not far from here."

"Llampha?"

"Yeah, that's the place," Ben said without missing a beat.

"Shall we call them? Get them to come and pick you up?"

I inhaled sharply, which wasn't a smart move because Phyllis looked at me and it felt like the chunk of beet might have shot down the wrong pipe.

Phyllis's crinkly brow got even crinklier. "Everything alright with Supergirl here?"

"She's fine." Ben patted me on the back and the beet found its way back into my mouth. I made sure I chewed it and swallowed it properly.

"Would you like me to call your parents?"

I opened my mouth a few times and then said, "Ummm ... ohhh ... errrr ..."

Ben was as cool as the cucumber-and-jam sandwiches that were left untouched in the middle of the table. "That would be great, but they're out walking for the day. We're going to get a bus."

He spoke so convincingly that *I* almost believed him.

"You won't get a bus coming through here again now. Not on a Sunday." Phyllis waved her scone as she spoke. A bit dropped off into her tea—it made a splash and sank. Like my hopes. We were never going to get to St. David's before somebody at home missed us.

I finally managed to get some actual words out. "So we're stuck here?"

"No, it's not far." Phyllis brushed the crumbs off her hands. "I'll drive you."

PC Mike's eyebrows shot up his forehead. "Out of the question. You're banned. That well that you almost destroyed was an historical landmark and three hundred years old."

"Do you have guacamole in your eyes too?" I asked but I don't think Phyllis heard me because she made this snorting noise and turned on PC Mike. "He's got spam patties where he should have brains. I'm an excellent driver."

PC Mike's face went purple. He banged both his fists on the table and the cups and plates jumped. "I will not be undermined in public, Aunty Phyllis."

They stared at each other for a minute. Charlie caught my eye and whispered, "Awkward."

Phyllis folded her arms across herself tightly. I was getting seriously-angry-old-lady vibes. As much as I already liked her, I was definitely siding with PC Mike—my experience of old lady drivers made me naturally cautious. I was not eager to get in a car driven by her—especially as she had ignored my question about the guacamole.

"If Mike had passed his driving test, he could have given you a police escort." Phyllis drained her tea and stood up. "But he hasn't, so he can't. Come on, boys, look alive. I've got something in the garage that might be of use."

We followed Phyllis back outside while PC Mike disappeared to write his (as it turned out) factually incorrect news article. She pulled open the doors to her garage and shouted, "Ta-da! They're yours if you want them. They'll get you to Llampha, no trouble."

In among the spider webs, plant pots, and lawnmower were an old canoe and a rowing machine. It was clear that Phyllis was a few cucumber-and-jam sandwiches short of a picnic. Ben, Charlie, and I all started giving each other these looks, which Phyllis must have seen because she said, "What do you think?"

I wanted to be delicate about it, so I said, "Wonderful, thank you, but we're not very good with a paddle."

Phyllis wasn't so delicate in her response. She said, "No, you dope, the bikes—I thought you could take the bikes."

That's when I spotted one very long bike and one very old-looking bike in the corner of the garage.

"The tandem bike takes some getting used to, but I'm sure you'll get the hang of it."

I started to make my way toward them. "You'd let us have these?"

"I don't use them. Not with my hips."

They weren't the coolest bikes in the world. I mean, the single bike had a wicker basket on the front *and* it was lilac with shiny pink tassels coming out of the handlebars. The tandem bike looked like it could have been around when woolly mammoths stomped the Earth. But they were transport.

"You'd better pump up the tires, but apart from that they're in pretty good shape."

That was clearly a matter of opinion, but I was not going to turn down some new wheels because of a patch of rust. I picked up the tandem bike. "It's very generous of you."

"You'll need helmets of course. I'll go and ask Mike to give you some of his police-issue ones. You practice riding that tandem around the garden."

She turned to leave but before she did I found myself

asking her a question. "How far is it from here to St. David's?"

"Why would you want to know a thing like that?"

"Curious, that's all."

"About a hundred miles," she said and disappeared into her house.

"A hundred miles." I slung my leg over the first seat of the tandem bike. A hundred miles wasn't *that* far. I just didn't know if the others would agree.

I opened my mouth but before I could speak Ben said, "You've got that look."

"What look?"

"The same look you had when you made us strip a family of scarecrows for their superhero costumes." Ben looked at me suspiciously and then said, "Oh no. No, no, no, no, no. You want us to bike to St. David's, don't you?"

"It's not a *terrible* idea," I said. "What do you think?"

I waited for Ben to answer while he looked up at the sky and blew air out of his cheeks.

"I think if I agree to bike a hundred miles to the most western coast of Wales, I'm not doing it on a purple bike with glittery tassels. That bike was made for Supergirl."

A little pulse of excitement rippled through me. He hadn't said no. "Okay, so if I take the purple bike, you'll do it?"

"I guess. If you really want to."

This was super-excellent news. "You're the best."

"I know." And then quietly he said, "I'm in no rush to go home yet."

An angry cough behind me made me remember that Ben wasn't the only person I needed to convince.

"So if Ben's the best, what does that make me?"

I looked at Charlie with my biggest begging eyes, pressed my hands together like I was praying, and dropped to my knees. "The equalist bestest wonderfullest friend ever?"

"Get up," he said, "and don't be weird. I'm in. The further away I am from Camp All Soy And No Joy, the better. But we probably should call home if we're going to be away for another night. Make up an excuse and let them know we're okay."

"That is some bestest wonderfullest forward thinking from my equalist bestest friend," I said.

"All brains, me," Charlie said and swung his leg over the back saddle seat of the tandem bike. And then he said, "Hey, where are the handlebars?"

Ben rolled his eyes. "Dude, you've mounted that backward."

17

This is where we meet Sheila

With Mike writing his report in one of the upstairs rooms and Phyllis out of earshot in the kitchen, we took the opportunity to call home from her landline. We all told the same lies—that we were staying over another night at our friend's and that our phones weren't working properly.

When Ben rang his house, Becky answered the phone. Ben said she didn't seem bothered he would be away longer, and that she sounded pleased more than anything. She had told him not to be a nuisance and then had hung up on him. Ben's face looked a little darker after the call.

One of Charlie's three sisters answered when he called home. There was a lot of noise in the background. After a lot of shouting, his mom eventually came to the phone, made him promise to make healthy choices and mind his manners, and told him that they would discuss what happened to his phone when he got back.

Dad answered the phone after the first ring. "Fred, I've just been trying to call. Everything okay?" I wasn't sure, but he sounded sad, which made it really hard to lie to him.

"Yeah, sorry, I broke my phone. You okay?"

"Fine—missing you though, bud."

I felt bad when he said that. "I miss you too . . ." I swallowed and then rushed the next bit: "But can I stay another night?"

There was a pause. "Course you can, son. If that's what you want."

"It's just that Ben and Charlie will be going away on their vacations soon." It wasn't a lie as such.

"I understand. Don't you worry about your old dad. Mr. Burnley's been around, keeping an eye on me."

"We'll have loads of time together later during break."

"Course we will, Fred. You go have fun with your friends."

"Thanks, Dad. Love you."

"Love you too, Fred."

"Look after yourself. Try and have a healthy breakfast."

I heard the *pssst* sound of a can being opened. "Proud of you, Fred."

I felt like the worst person in the world.

Ben must have figured there was something wrong because he asked if I was okay as soon as I'd hung up.

"I'm fine," I said. "You okay?"

Ben nodded, but the way he said, "Yeah, you know how it is," made me think he wasn't fine. At all.

It was after noon by the time we finally set off from Phyllis's house on our new-old bikes. Having earlier pelted Albert and Mike with potato and pear, she didn't have any ingredients left to make us some more of her turnovers. Instead, she insisted on giving us the leftover cucumber-and-jam sandwiches for the journey. I thought they'd be awful, but they were actually alright.

PC Mike shouted his goodbyes from upstairs. He sounded very excited when we left. As we pulled away, we heard him shout something that sounded like, "Seven hundred likes already, it's a record. It's a miracle, Aunty Phyllis!"

It wasn't a miracle—it was the power of the internet combined with a much exaggerated superhero story, but I didn't know what he was talking about at the time. We found out later though.

As we got down to pedaling, I made sure the other two knew the plan. "We need to cycle as far as we can before it gets dark and then we can find a hotel or one of those youth hostel places for the night."

Ben said, "As long as *something* isn't a boat."

I checked the money in my underpants. "We've got

around forty quid. I figure we can cover a hundred miles easy in one and a half days."

Obviously, I figured wrong, but at the time I had absolute faith in our cycling ability. I think there's something about wearing a superhero costume that gives you an unwavering sense of self-confidence.

By the time we were halfway up the first hill, Ben realized his mistake in giving me the lilac bike. He was having to work twice as hard to shift Charlie's body weight.

He kept shouting, "Are you sure you're pedaling back there?"

To which Charlie would say, "Busting a gut, mate," even though I could see he was relaxing while Ben did all the legwork.

I was going to tell Ben but then he said, "Don't know why you're smiling, Supergirl," so I kept my mouth shut and sped off to the top of the hill.

And that's where I saw a truly surprising sight. There was a sheep lying on its back in the middle of the road, its four legs pointing skyward.

By the time Charlie and Ben made it to the top of the hill, I'd propped my bike against a bush and was standing over the sheep, wondering what to do. Panting, Ben brought the tandem bike to a stop beside me.

Charlie had this look of utter horror on his face. "Fred! What did you do to that sheep?"

"*I* didn't do anything to it. I just found it here."

Ben climbed off his bike and bent down to get a closer look. "Is it alive?"

The sheep wiggled its legs a little, like it was using up the last of its strength.

"Yes, it is! But it doesn't look particularly spritely."

"Where do you think it came from?" Charlie looked up, as though he thought it had fallen from the heavens.

"Well, not from up there! We have to turn it over. I read in a fact book that sheep can't right themselves once they're on their backs."

Charlie frowned. "You read some really weird stuff, Fred."

Ben crouched down on the ground. "Come on then. It's time to be heroic! Spidey, Supergirl, grab a handful of sheep and heave."

Considering that sheep look a bit like fluffy white clouds, I was not prepared for how heavy the thing was. I didn't think we were going to manage it, but like all good superheroes, we didn't give up and eventually the sheep was back on all fours.

"Go on, Sheila," Charlie said. "Off you go, go find your family."

"Sheila?" Ben said.

"She looks like a Sheila, don't you think?"

I shrugged. "I guess."

Sheila dipped her head in what I like to think was her saying, *Thank you, brave superheroes*, and then disappeared off into the fields through a hole in the fence. We got back on our bikes, feeling more than a little proud of our efforts.

It felt like we had been cycling forever by the time we reached the next village. My butt was sore, I had these weird yellow bumps forming on my hands, my legs were tired, and my costume was damp with sweat. Exhausted, we threw our bikes down on the green outside the village shop. By my reckoning we'd probably covered at least thirty miles. We bought three cans of orange soda and three candy bars for a snack, and I set about asking the shop owner as to our exact whereabouts.

The shopkeeper was a whiskery man with a face like a turnip. As I slid a fiver across the counter I said, "Excuse me, sir, do you have the time?"

He didn't look up from the little TV set he was watching. "It's almost two o'clock."

That didn't make sense. We couldn't have been cycling for less than two hours.

"How far are we from Gileston?"

"Just over five miles as the bird flies."

"Is that all?"

He handed me our change. "Sorry, love, can't make it any longer."

I turned to Ben and Charlie. "That means we're traveling at about three miles an hour. We could have walked faster."

"It was very hilly," Charlie said.

"And windy," Ben said.

"And there was Sheila," Charlie added.

"Do you know how long it's going to take us to cycle a hundred miles?"

"Three hundred hours!" Charlie leaned against the counter. "I can't sit on that saddle for three hundred hours."

"Just over thirty-three hours, Charlie, you doofus," Ben said a bit uncharitably. "But it's still a long time."

Charlie's never been the best at math, but he is really good at languages. He even made up his own one in fourth year. Spent a whole term talking to us in Charlish.

The shop bell clanged behind us as I closed the door. "We're never going to cycle another forty-five miles today and fifty tomorrow. What was I thinking?"

"Cheer up. Superheroes don't mope." Ben opened his soda next to my face and it sprayed in my eyes. "We just need to adjust the plan, that's all. Come up with a super-plan."

18

We accidentally do something that looks a bit heroic-ish

We lay on the grass, looking up at the clouds, and tried to think of a super-plan—but before we could come up with anything, the shop owner burst through the door, shouting and pointing his stubby finger at us. "It is you, isn't it? The outfits—they're the same. It's you, I know it is!"

We turned around to check if he was talking to somebody behind us, but we were the only people around.

Charlie swallowed the last of his candy bar. "What do you mean, it's *you*?"

The shopkeeper was jumping from foot to foot, his face flushed pink. "Come in and see. Come quick!"

We followed him back into the shop. He pointed at the TV screen and clapped his pudgy hands together. "See, it is you, isn't it?"

I froze.

He was right. It was us. On *South Wales Today*. Sitting on top of Albert.

"When you came in here I didn't know you were genuine superheroes. I thought you were just kids in costumes."

I was barely listening, because PC Mike had appeared on the screen. A woman in a bright blue suit and fluffy hair like a cloud held a microphone under his huge smiling mouth.

"I'm here with Mike Griffiths, the journalist who broke this miraculous good-news story. How many hits have you had since you put the story on Twitter?"

"Just over half a million in a few hours."

"Half a million!" I shouted. It was hard to believe news had traveled so quickly, but the internet is a powerful thing. We later discovered the fluffy-hair woman was PC Mike's second cousin. When he contacted her, she was over to his place in a flash, asking him questions like, "What do you think it is about this super-trio that has captured the country's imagination?"

"So much, Carys. First, their bravery. The picture shows only one of the attackers, but they were outnumbered by ten to three—it's a miracle really—"

This was the first of PC Mike's humongous whoppers. As if there were even ten other people in Gileston.

"Second, they seemed to possess a superhuman strength—"

I mean . . . what?! The lies just seemed to trip off his tongue.

"And third, they appeared out of nowhere and then vanished just as quickly."

Nothing about that bike ride felt quick.

"So we have no idea who these superheroes are?"

I held my breath.

"I believe one of them goes by the name of Charlie Ow. That's all I have."

"Thank you, Mike." The fluffy-haired woman turned to face the camera. "I think we can all sleep better in our beds knowing there are some real-life superheroes out there protecting us. If you see them, please let us know. We'd love to talk to them! Now back to the studio."

We stood staring at the screen while the weatherman told us it was going to remain hot and sunny with a small chance of superhero showers.

The flash of a camera snapped me out of my trance.

Dazzled, I said, "What are you doing, Mr. Shopkeeper, sir?"

"I'm tweeting this photo to *South Wales Today*. Real superheroes in my shop—think what it will do for business." He disappeared behind the counter.

My instincts told me this was not a good idea, so I ran after him shouting, "We're not real superheroes, honest."

"Yes, you are."

"No, we're not!"

"If Carys Griffiths from *South Wales Today* says you are, and I say you are, then you are, okay?"

It wasn't okay because it wasn't the truth, but I had a feeling that he wasn't too bothered about that.

Unfortunately, what happened next didn't exactly help my argument, as we ended up looking very superhero-ish by complete accident.

There was a low grumbling sound outside that made the shop windows vibrate. Outside, a person dressed all in leather had pulled up on a motorcycle. He looked like a Power Ranger who had gone to the dark side. I immediately thought it was the Gaffer and every muscle in my body clenched. In truth, I had such a violent whole-body reaction that I managed to give myself a wedgie. I think my butt must have contracted so hard that it temporarily swallowed part of my costume.

I watched terrified and slightly uncomfortable as the person got off the motorcycle and headed for the door of the shop. There was no time to hide. No time to run. Things were about to turn bad. Very bad. I knew this because of the following:

Clue 1: The biker did not remove his helmet after entering the shop.

Clue 2: He was holding a gun.

Clue 3: He said, "Good afternoon, ladies and
gentlemen. If you would be so kind as to remain
calm during the duration of this robbery, that
would be most appreciated."

I have to say, as far as robbers go, he was very polite. It sort of made you want to do as he asked. However, it turned out that the shopkeeper was not one for following instructions. He passed out immediately. We probably all should have done the same, but as it was, we remained one hundred percent conscious.

"Are you the Gaffer?" I stammered.

The helmet turned to me. "Who?"

I gulped. "Never mind."

We weren't being robbed by the Gaffer. We were being robbed by a completely different criminal. This, while not at the top of my list of things to do on a Sunday, did make me feel a little better.

The robber threw a duffle bag at Charlie. "Spiderman—may I call you Spiderman?"

Charlie didn't answer.

"I'll take that as a yes. Spiderman, may I trouble you to fill this with the contents of the register?"

Charlie didn't reply, he just stood there looking scared and whimpering, which seemed like a reasonable thing to do in the circumstances.

"I'd like to take this opportunity to remind you that this is a gun and it is loaded."

Ben gulped. I gulped. Charlie whimpered a little louder.

"So if you wouldn't mind opening the register."

There was an awkward pause and Ben had to nudge Charlie, who eventually jerked into action, stepped behind the counter, and rattled the register drawer. "I can't. It's locked. I don't know how."

"Could I trouble you to try again? Perhaps with a little more conviction?"

Charlie banged the register harder, then picked it up and gave it a good shake. "You can trouble me all you want, but it's not opening."

"I'm afraid it just won't do to leave here empty-handed." The robber didn't sound impressed and I couldn't help feeling that we were letting him down.

"Let me try." Ben sidled next to Charlie and began pressing all the buttons on the cash register.

By now the robber was getting antsy, so I asked myself, *What would Supergirl do?* As I didn't think I could bicycle-kick the gun out of his hands, I thought I could use my powers of persuasion instead, so I said, "Look, if it won't open you could always help yourself to some chocolate bars instead?"

My suggestion didn't go over too well because he said,

"I'm not going to get very far on chocolate bars, miss. Now would someone please open the register before things become rather *unpleasant*."

The atmosphere was getting tense. He clearly wasn't going to leave until we had given him what he wanted, but the register would not open. Even when we dropped it on the floor.

Just when things looked like they might get *unpleasant*, Ben said, "What about this? It's not money but it's better than a chocolate bar." He stuffed his hand down his costume. I had NO clue what he was about to pull out.

"It's pure gold. Priceless. Been on the *Antiques Roadshow* and everything."

My mouth fell open. Ben was holding one of the swan rings. I said, "Ben! You took that?"

He shrugged. "Thought we might need some collateral."

"Why would we need collateral?"

"Oh, I don't know. Maybe if we find ourselves in the middle of a hold-up situation."

In the circumstances, I couldn't really argue.

"Marvelous, that will do nicely." The robber plucked the ring from Ben's hand and held it up to the light to examine it. He must have liked what he saw because he tried to slip it into his pocket, but his leather pants were too tight, so he gave up and said, "A pleasure doing business with you."

He waved his gun at us one more time and then disappeared out of the door. I heard the sound of the motorcycle engine and the squeal of tires on asphalt and he was gone.

After a few seconds I said, "Well, as far as hold-ups go, that wasn't too bad."

Ben kind of crumpled onto the floor like a deflating balloon and Charlie grabbed a giant chocolate bar from the shelf and bit into it without even taking the wrapper off.

The shop owner must have sensed it was a good time to come around, because he suddenly popped up from behind the counter and said, "Has he gone?"

Ben said, "Yeah, he's gone."

I wanted to say, *No thanks to you.*

The shopkeeper scrambled over to the cash register and pushed a button on the side and the drawer sprang open. And we all went, "Ahhhhh, that's how it opens."

"It's all there! He didn't take any money?"

"No, he didn't take any money," Ben said.

The shopkeeper turned to us, this strange look of awe in his eyes, and said, "It's a miracle! You truly are superheroes."

I could have tried to set him straight there and then, but I knew it would be a waste of time. And he was so grateful. I mean, *really* grateful. He kept shaking our hands and thanking us over and over again. He called us his miraculous superheroes so many times, we almost started to believe it. I guess, even though there had been no bicycle-kicks or shows of superhuman strength, a teeny tiny part of us felt like superheroes just for surviving.

The shopkeeper gave us a box of candy as a reward and as Ben was putting it into the basket of my bike he said to me, "You know what, Fred, if we can find a way out of a hold-up situation, chances are that we'll be able to find Alan Froggley."

And Charlie said, "Yeah, nothing can stop us."

And you know what? I thought so too.

19

I end up sulking about our whole situation and take it out on my cape

Midway through sixth year, Mrs. Walker had a huge rant about the importance of having a protractor and pinned a sign to our classroom door that said, *By failing to prepare, you are preparing to fail*, or something like that. At the time I couldn't see why protractors were such a big deal, but as I sat on the green outside the shop with our long bike ride to St. David's ahead of us, I had an epiphany. Mrs. Walker wasn't just talking about math equipment. She was talking about life.

Although now that we were part-superhero and I was feeling more confident about our chances of getting to St. David's, I thought that perhaps some preparation might be a good idea. While Ben and Charlie had a little snooze in the sun, I decided to do a full assessment of our situation. And this is when I realized the following worrying facts:

1. A criminal had taken our stolen ring.
2. He'd probably try and sell it on the black market.
3. News of this might reach the Gaffer.
4. The Gaffer could find out the ring came from three kids dressed as superheroes in Llampha.
5. It was only a matter of time before the Gaffer would come for us.

By the time I had swallowed the little sick burp that had taken me by surprise, I knew we had to get going fast.

I gave Ben and Charlie a kick to wake them up.

Charlie sat up looking all confused. "You okay, Fred? You don't look so great."

I didn't feel great, but I had to focus on practical things. "We need to go, right now."

"Can't we just—"

"No, we're leaving, and we need to find a change of clothes."

"You pee in your costume too?" Charlie asked.

"Ewww! No, I didn't."

Ben grinned at me. "It's okay if you did. It was pretty scary."

"I'm telling you, I didn't." I might have done a teeny dribble, but he didn't need to know that.

Charlie said, "No, me neither," but I couldn't help

noticing a slightly darker patch around Spiderman's crotch.

"We can sort out clothes later, but we need to get out of here, like, *now*."

"What's the rush?" Ben asked.

"If that guy tells anyone where he got that stolen ring, the Gaffer might come looking for us and it's not like we're difficult to spot. I don't see many other kids dressed as superheroes around here."

Ben's face went pale. "I . . . I didn't think of that."

"Which is why we need to go."

Charlie didn't have to be told twice—he was up and pedaling before Ben had a chance to swing his leg over the saddle. Fortunately for Ben, it's difficult to steer a tandem bike from the back seat, so Charlie didn't get very far before he crashed to the ground.

Ben wasn't happy that he'd been left behind. "You tried to leave me! You . . . you . . . abandoner!"

Charlie scrambled out from under the bike. "Sorry, dude, I panicked."

Ben shook his head. "Maybe you could try and put that sort of effort into pedaling when we're on a hill?"

We headed out of Llampha with no clear idea of where we were going, apart from as far away from the scene of the robbery as possible. Mrs. Walker probably would have considered this as failing to prepare.

After our initial high-speed burst, our pace dropped, and I took more notice of where we were headed. We kept to the small roads as I thought we'd have less chance of being noticed. And I was right. The roads got smaller and smaller until they were more like tracks. After about an hour of cycling deeper into the countryside, we hadn't seen a soul. In fact, we didn't come across any sign of life other than a lot of sheep. Naturally, Charlie thought every one he saw was Sheila.

I got a little worried, but I didn't let on to Ben or Charlie that I hadn't a clue where we were. After we cycled past some very familiar looking sheep for a third time, I had all the evidence I needed to prove we were pedaling in circles. I kept this nugget of information to myself for another half an hour but then my anxiety—and the chafing of Lycra, bottom flesh, and bicycle seat—became too much for me to bear. I pulled into a field to 'fess up to Charlie and Ben that we were completely and utterly lost in deepest darkest Wales.

I leaned my bike against a fence and slumped down onto the grass. My cape got caught on a nail and it strangled me. Being attacked by my own clothing was too much of an insult, so I pulled my cape off and tried to rip it. Whoever invented Lycra knew what they were doing—it is surprisingly hard to tear. That only made me angrier. I went into full-on tantrum mode. I threw it on the ground and jumped on it. Again and again.

Once I was certain that the cape was not going to attack me anymore, I picked it up and threw it over the hedge and then collapsed on the ground.

"Not your color?" Ben said as he sat down next to me.

"I think we should go home." My words surprised me but as soon as they were out of my mouth, I knew I meant them. Everything was a disaster.

Ben nudged me gently with his shoulder. "You don't mean that."

"I do. I really do. We're lost and miles from St. David's, we're probably being hunted by a criminal called the Gaffer, and our parents will ground us for life once they find out about all this, which they will."

"I know—exciting, isn't it?"

"That's one word for it," Charlie said.

Obviously, Ben had lost the plot. It wasn't exciting. It was terrifying.

But Ben didn't see it that way. "Fred, you can't give up now."

"Can't I?"

"Look, it's pretty obvious that finding Alan Froggley is important to you. And I don't think you should give up on things that are important. Some people quit too easily.

When things get tough, they just up and disappear off to Spain."

Ben was clearly working through some stuff of his own. I nudged him back with my shoulder. "You okay, mate?"

He picked up a stone and chucked it over the wall. Then he shook his head and gave me a weak smile. "Okay, so some of that was more about me, but still, you shouldn't give up. Supergirl wouldn't."

"Oh, ha ha." I sighed a really big sigh. "I don't know, Ben. All the signs seem to be clearly telling us to quit before we die or end up in a juvenile detention center for the rest of our lives."

"You can't be in a juvenile detention center for the rest of your life. They'd move you to a grown-up facility at some point," Charlie said.

"Not the time, Spidey," Ben said and then fixed his eyes back on me. "Fred, come on, dude, what about the signs that are telling us we should keep going?"

I couldn't help it, I laughed when he said that. "You want to tell me what signs are telling us to keep going?"

"Look." Ben pointed at Charlie.

"Charlie?"

Ben had this funny twinkly look in his eyes. "Not Charlie—look at what he's eating."

I still wasn't getting it. But I *was* concerned that Charlie was already plowing through our reward candy from the shop. For all I knew they might have been our last meal before we starved to death in the Welsh wilds.

"But *what* is he eating?"

Ben wasn't dropping it, so I said, "He's demolishing our box of Freddo Frog bars."

Ben's smile grew wider. "Freddo Frogs. Don't you see, Fred? That's you. Freddo Froggley? It's not a sign, it's . . ." He paused and looked at Charlie. "How many in there, mate?"

Charlie turned the box around. "Sixty minus three . . . okay, minus six."

"There are fifty-four signs that you, Freddo Frog, should continue on your quest to find your biological father." Ben folded his arms and nodded triumphantly.

I think he wanted me to say something meaningful, but all I said was, "Freddie Froggley? Freddie Froggley?" like it was a question.

I couldn't be Freddie Froggley. High school was going to be hard enough as it was with a regular name, let alone being named after Cadbury's cheapest chocolate bar. But before I could get completely devastated by this bomb-shell, Ben jumped to his feet and began singing.

To start with, I thought, *Why is he singing at a totally terrible time like this?* And then I realized what he was singing. He was singing "One More Step Along the World I Go." But instead of *step* he was singing *hop* and instead of *traveling* he sang *ribbiting*. Which I think was his attempt at some frog-based humor. I guess it was pretty funny.

It didn't take long for Charlie to join in. It was a clever song choice by Ben—it was both personal and motivating. They pulled me to my feet and I sang along with them. When we finished the last verse, we started again and we danced around that field somewhere in South Wales singing and croaking and laughing until Charlie did a little bit of chocolate puke down his Spiderman costume. That was one bodily fluid too many. We really had to get a change of clothes.

20

We end up sleeping in a church and I learn facts about pigs and shrimp

Fueled by just over ten chocolate amphibians each and on aching bowed legs due to three cases of serious saddle-bottom, Ben and I pushed the bikes through a field of sheep while Charlie kept trying to spot Sheila. Ben thought he had seen a building. After we stood on top of a gate for a better look, Charlie and I decided Ben might be right. We hoped that a building might mean people, or a phone, or a change of clothes at least.

In reality the building meant pews, a font, and an organ. We'd found a church in the middle of a field in the middle of nowhere.

"Three Saints Church," Charlie read aloud.

The clock on the steeple told us it was five thirty. The day was disappearing, we were tired and seriously saddle-sore, so, like all good leaders, I made a decision. "Let's see if we can stay here for the night. Get some rest and then start out again in the morning. What do you think?" I was worried about how they might react. After all, I was asking them to spend another night away from home and on the run from the Gaffer.

Charlie hugged me. He did not smell good, but I was so pleased he was okay with everything that I didn't mention it and just breathed through my mouth.

"Fred, that sounds like a fantastic idea. My butt and that bike have fallen out big time."

"I'm up for a rest," Ben said and pushed the door open.

I followed him inside and called out, "Hello?" and crossed my fingers that there would be no answer.

My finger-crossing worked—the place was deserted. I felt the hairs on the back of my arms prickle under my Lycra. "It's cold in here."

"It is a little chilly," Ben said, wrapping his cape around him. I wished I hadn't lost my cool and stomped mine into the dirt.

I found a light switch and flicked it on. "Let's take a look around."

At the back of the church, near the door where we had come in, was a table covered in a white cloth. On it was a big leather-bound book that told the story of Three Saints Church.

I ran my finger along the writing. It was all twirly like Grams's. "Says here Three Saints Church was built in 1766 in honor of three Welsh saints, Cian, Dynod, and Elvis—"

"Let me have a look." Ben pushed in next to me. "There's no way there was a Saint Elvis."

I shoved him out of the way. "Whoever wrote this seemed to think there was. Now listen—Saint Cian was made a saint because he spoke nothing but the Lord's words, day and night, for thirty years."

"Bet he was popular," Charlie said as he sat down in the last pew.

"Saint Dynod, well, he was a *man of ample proportions.* He was made a saint because he carried the villagers of Llampha to safety during the great flood."

Charlie rested his chin on the back of the pew. "And Saint Elvis? What did he do?"

I skim-read Elvis's entry because it was a huge passage that went on about the earth and soil and fertilization and seeds. "Basically, he was good at gardening."

Charlie scoffed. "You can be a saint for being good at gardening?"

"Apparently so."

"Why isn't Mr. Bloom from that gardening show one then?"

"Well, maybe he will be when he's dead," Ben said.

I turned the page. "Hey, listen to this. The bodies of the Three Saints went missing from the crypt and were never found. When the bones were here, this church used to be a place of pilgrimage."

"What's 'pilgrimage' again?" Charlie asked.

I wasn't sure, but I don't like not knowing an answer, so I made an educated guess. "Something that pilgrims do?"

Charlie frowned. "Those tiny sardines?"

Ben laughed. "No, those are pilchards. Pilgrimage is when people go on a religious vacation. Like a resort but with more praying."

"Exactly," I said and continued reading. "When the Saints disappeared in the 1900s, so did the pilgrims. And the church kind of got forgotten about. That's sad."

"Poor church," Charlie said, rubbing his pew.

Ben set off down the central aisle. "Come on, let's go explore before Charlie forms too close a relationship with the furniture."

At the far end was a table with a cross on it and a statue of Jesus. There were some steps up to the pulpit— that's the place where the minister stands to talk at the congregation—and two rows of pews where the choir would sit. Charlie walked straight up the steps.

"What are you doing?" I said. "Only special people are allowed up there."

Charlie grinned. "If Spiderman isn't special, I don't know who is."

"No, seriously, don't you have to be blessed by a priest or by God to be in that part of the church?"

"What do you think's going to happen?"

"You could be smited."

"What's that?"

I wasn't one hundred percent certain but said, "When God strikes you down."

"With what?"

"I dunno, something from the sky, like a lightning bolt."

Out of nowhere a really loud, deep sound filled the church and I thought we might be getting a firsthand example of what smiting was.

Charlie leaped down the steps and grabbed me. I tried to dodge out of the way—if he was being smited for trespassing on holy ground I didn't want him dangling off me. But I was too slow, and he ended up clinging onto my back like a baby chimpanzee. I spun around furiously to try and get him off. I only stopped spinning when I heard Ben laughing.

"Look at you two!"

And then another sound reverberated through the church. Different this time—almost jolly. Definitely familiar.

Ben was sitting at the church organ, playing his fourth year piano piece, "The Entertainer."

I peeled Charlie off me. "Ben, cut it out, someone will hear!"

"Chill out, Fred. Who's going to complain—a load of sheep? There's no one around for miles." He switched to "Chopsticks" and flashed me his scrunchy-face smile. Which really wound me up.

"Just quit messing around. And it's a flock, fluff-for-brains."

"What?"

"It's a flock of sheep. Not a load."

"Whatever, Bo Peep." He wagged his head from side to side and then said, *"It's a flock,"* in this high-pitched voice that was supposed to sound like mine but didn't.

He hammered the keys harder and shouted over to Charlie, "Two parts?"

And then there were two of them banging away. When Charlie said, "Again from the top," I got mad and left them to it. While they messed around, I was going to be useful and explore the church.

Halfway through a very clunky version of "Old MacDonald" I found a door that led into a little room. It was probably where the priest or minister went to do his private praying. Inside was a desk, a closet, and a cabinet. After a thorough search I had found the following items:

1. A big box of communion wafers with a best-before date of August 1998
2. A pen with *Jesus is all-write by me* on the side
3. A box of matches
4. A massive candle
5. Twelve white robe things choirboys wear, which I have since learned are called cassocks.

I headed back into the main part of the church just as Ben and Charlie were claiming there was a pterodactyl on Old MacDonald's farm. I was pretty pleased with my hoard.

"Look what I've got," I shouted over "*a rooooar-rooooar there.*" "New clothes." I held up three white robes. "While you two have been playing, I've been doing something useful."

Charlie said, "You found some choirboys and stripped them?"

I sighed. "No. These robes were hanging up in a closet. Brilliant, huh?"

Ben didn't look very impressed. "You want us to wear those?"

"Yes, I want us to wear those. We can't risk the superhero costumes any longer. What if the Gaffer is looking for us?"

"Yeah but—"

"And I'm sorry, Charlie, but you stink." It was a bit harsh, but it was true.

"You don't exactly smell like Febreze either, dude."

"So let's change."

I looked at them. It was so obvious that they knew I was right.

"Fine." Ben pulled off the top half of his Batman outfit. "We should wash first."

I had already thought of this but there was a problem. "I found a toilet and a sink at the back but when you turn on the faucet it makes a horrible groaning noise and this nasty brown water rushes out."

"What about the font?" Ben said.

I wasn't sure about that idea. "Holy water—can we use it? Isn't that kind of powerful?"

"What do you think is going to happen? That you'll sprout wings?"

"I don't know how these religious things work," I said.

The font was the most impressive part of the church. There was a plaque that said its water was pumped from a holy spring. That had to be top-grade holy water. But what I liked most was the statue of the Virgin Mary that rose from the base. Even though she was carved from stone, she had a kind face. She didn't look like the sort who would mind us using the water to wash our armpits.

It felt good to peel off our costumes. Mine had gone crinkly in places. When I put on the cassock it felt like I was wearing a petal.

I twirled around. "Perfect—loose, comfortable, and yet still provides enough warmth."

Ben only grunted. It wouldn't have hurt him to show a little gratitude.

After we'd finished the rest of the Freddo Frogs and the communion wafers (which tasted like flying saucers without the flying bit), Charlie went to use the facilities. That's a polite way of saying he needed to do a number two. Ben and I popped outside for a pee, which is trickier than you think in a cassock. The night sky was even more amazing than it had been in Barry. I pointed out the Milky Way. You can only see it in dark places. There's too much light pollution in big cities, but in that churchyard in South Wales, we had an awesome view.

"Did you know that two million years ago, early man would have seen the light from a supermassive black hole in the Milky Way," I said.

"What *is* a black hole?" Ben asked.

"It's what left when a big star explodes. It sort of collapses in on itself and the gravity inside is mega and it becomes super powerful and sucks stuff into it." I know this because for my tenth birthday Dad gave me a book called *The Night Sky: 500 Amazing Facts.* In the front he'd written, *Amazing facts for my amazing son.*

"The more I look, the more stars I see," Ben said.

"Makes you feel small and insignificant, doesn't it— all those stars, all that sky?"

"Don't need to look at the stars to feel like that," Ben said in a very small voice.

We went back inside, and while we waited for Charlie to finish doing his business, we took all the pew cushions into the little room and made this huge bed for us to sleep on. We turned out the lights and lit the big candle. Ben checked where the fire extinguisher was kept in case we experienced another incident like that on the boat.

I lay down and covered myself with one of the spare cassocks. I stretched back and closed my eyes. "This is actually pretty comfortable."

"Better than my bed at home." Ben commando-rolled next to me. "And the bonus is that there's no Becky."

"Is she really that bad?"

Ben didn't answer to start with.

I opened one eye and watched his chest expand upward as he did this great big sigh.

"My dad doesn't notice me when she's around."

"You should talk to him about it. Let him know how you feel."

"It's not like I haven't tried. He makes all these promises about spending time together—just us—but it never happens."

"Have you tried talking to Becky about it?"

"Are you kidding? She's the problem."

"If she's the problem then maybe she's the solution too."

Ben propped himself up on his elbow and studied my face. "Fred, are you suggesting . . . because I have this plan . . . to get rid of—"

At that moment, I was fairly certain Ben was about to admit to plotting to kill Becky. "No, Ben! No! Murder is not the answer."

He picked up a pew cushion and bashed me around the head with it. My eyes rattled like a pea on a spoon. Those things are much heavier than you realize.

"I don't want to kill Becky, doofus."

"That's good to hear. But if you change your mind you could definitely use one of these cushions to whack her with. They're like bricks."

"I was thinking of a way to get rid of Dad's money. I'm sure that's all she's interested in. When the money's gone, she'll follow."

It seemed like sound enough reasoning.

"I can help you out with that if you want. I don't mind spending all your dad's cash. Think of it as a thank you for coming with me to find Alan Froggley."

"You thought about what you're going to say to him when we find him?"

"A little . . . A lot . . . Oh, I don't know. Maybe something like, 'Nice to meet you, I'm your son, Freddie'?"

"Are you worried how your other dad is going to feel? He's a good guy, Mom says."

"I am massively worried about how my dad's going to feel. I don't want to upset him. He *is* a good dad—the best. And I'm not trying to replace him or anything like that."

"So why then?"

It was hard to put into words. "I don't know *anyone* I'm related to. Not one person. If something happens to Dad, and chances are it will, I'm on my own. I can't let that happen. I need more people. I need more family."

"Nothing's going to happen to your dad."

"You can't know that. People die, Ben. They die all the time." It was a gloomy thing to say but it was the truth. I clenched my teeth together and tried to ignore the supermassive hole that was opening up inside me. I didn't want to think about dying. Or dead people. Like Grams. Or Mom. I had to focus on finding Alan.

We sat in silence for a while.

And then Ben said, "Did you know it is a genuine fact that it is physically impossible for a pig to look up into the sky."

I turned to him and said, "What?"

"I read it on a yogurt container once." He looked over at the window. "Imagine never seeing the stars and then being slapped between some bread, lettuce, and tomato."

It came out of nowhere, so I said, "What?" again.

"No matter how bad things get at least we're not pigs. At least we can look up and see the stars."

I was completely confused but I heard myself saying, "Yeah, at least we're not pigs."

"I don't remember many facts—not like you. But that one kind of stuck with me. Thought you might like it to add to your collection."

"Thanks."

"You're welcome."

I don't know whether it was because Ben's fact had filled up a bit of the black hole inside me . . . Or maybe it was just because he was there . . . Or maybe I was just happy I wasn't a pig . . . But whatever it was, I didn't feel so hollow anymore.

And then he said, "Actually, I've thought of another. Did you know a shrimp's heart is in its head?"

I laughed. "Really?" This was more brand-new information.

"Crazy, isn't it?"

"Where are you getting all these from?"

"It was a four-pack of yogurt. Don't remember the other two facts though. Was kind of blown away by the pig thing."

They sounded like excellent yogurt containers. I made a mental note to put them on the shopping list when I got back home. I was about to ask the brand when Charlie burst into the room. He was drenched.

"Who said yogurt? I'm starving."

He'd been gone so long I'd kind of forgotten about him. "Everything alright, Charlie?"

Ben snickered. "Your cassock's gone a bit see-through. I can see your nipples."

Charlie wrapped his arms around himself and blew a clump of damp hair out of his face. "No, Fred. Everything is not alright. Besides my deep soul-sapping hunger, I've had a slight situation in the toilet."

This was not good. Charlie had a situation in the toilet in third year. The boys had to use the girls' bathroom for the rest of the day until Dyno-Rod Drain Services arrived.

"It was probably those pear-and-potato turnovers. They were really heavy. Could sink a battleship. It was almost the size of a battleship." He plopped himself down between us. "Had to use a broom handle in the end. I think that's what broke the system."

"The system?" I said.

"Yeah, the pipes at the back of the toilet. Don't look so

worried, it's fixed now. The back pressure blew the taps off, but I found a little handle and when I turned it, the water stopped. But then it started again. So I wiggled it some more and I think that did the trick. I mean, it's making some weird noises but there's no *major* damage. Right—is there any?"

We looked at him blankly.

"Yogurt, I mean."

21

When Charlie tells us about
Jesus and the leopards

We managed to get a decent night's sleep on our bed of prayer cushions. The sun streamed through the window in the little room and woke us up early. Even though we thought it was very unlikely anyone would be around, we wanted to get away before most of Wales was awake.

We'd found a map of the area pinned to a bulletin board outside, next to a poster for a diet club from 1997. We figured out that we were only a few miles from the nearest village, but we decided to keep cycling until we got to a bigger one called Tythegston eight miles down the road. We could stop there for breakfast, make some phone calls home, and work out how to get to St. David's on just over thirty-five quid. We all agreed that we weren't going to make the full distance on our bikes. We thought maybe we could try and sell them to raise enough money for train fare.

We'd made sure to put all the cushions back and tidied up the place so it was just as we found it. There were some low, grumbling, clanking noises coming from the pipes. They were probably still trying to process Phyllis's pear-and-potato turnovers.

Riding a bike dressed as a choirboy isn't easy. We draped the cassocks over the handlebars to stop them from getting caught in the pedals and to keep our hands warm. And then we were off. There was a low-lying mist in the churchyard and Ben thought it would be funny to make *ooooooh* noises like he was a ghost or something. Let's just say, we found out later it wasn't the best idea he'd ever had.

We stuck to our plan and cycled right through the first village and up through the hills toward the next. It was a beautiful morning and it felt good to be alive. We sang all the best hymns from school, like the one that goes "Who put the hump upon the camel?" and "One More Step Along the World I Go." I think we were feeling the aftereffects of sleeping in a place of Our Lord and bathing in holy water.

A couple of miles into the journey we met a convoy of TV vans from *South Wales Today*, BBC, ITV, *and* Channel 4 on a particularly narrow road. Charlie panicked, fell off his bike, and ripped his cassock. We were too busy laughing because we could see his SpongeBob Square-Pants boxers to even consider that the vans might have had something to do with us.

It felt like we were making pretty good time. We'd only had two pee stops and I was beginning to feel like everything was going miraculously well for a change.

And then we saw the taxi.

Ben spotted it first when he turned around to check whether Charlie was actually pedaling. Their bike suddenly screeched to a halt and I almost got a face full of SpongeBob.

I was about to mouth off about being more considerate to other road users—meaning me—when Ben pointed a shaky finger over my shoulder and said, "Fred, mate, is that a taxi?"

It was a little ways off, but there was no mistaking the big black T painted on the white hood.

"Yeah, Ben, it is," I said in a quivery voice.

Charlie let out this weird wobbly noise that sounded a bit like a crazed turkey and grabbed hold of his tummy. At the time, I didn't think anything of it. Now I know he was a secret smuggler, but we didn't find out about that until later.

Ben looked at me with big buggy eyes. "You think it

might be—" He didn't finish—instead he did this big gulp like he was swallowing some puke—so I filled in what we were all thinking.

"The Gaffer?"

"Yup, the Gaffer." Ben gulped again.

I kicked down on my pedal. "I suggest we don't hang around to find out. Let's get a move on."

We started off down the road as quick as we could. I tried to convince myself that just because there was a taxi with a T on the hood like the one from Barry didn't mean it was the Gaffer, but it turns out I'm not very good at being convincing.

Every time I looked over my shoulder the taxi seemed to get closer, which I guess made sense, because the taxi had an engine and we just had our legs. I kept shouting to the others to keep going but it was pretty obvious the taxi was going to catch us.

I looked for an escape route. Tall thick hedges lined both sides of the road and I couldn't see any other turnoffs we could take ahead of us. Essentially, we were trapped. I remembered the gun we'd seen on the boat and realized we were either about to get sprayed with bullets or be run over like bowling pins. Come to think of it, we did look a bit like bowling pins in our cassocks.

The engine behind us growled and we all screamed.

I turned around and saw a bald man in the driver's seat. He looked like he'd walked right off the set of *The Sopranos*.

Charlie did not help my panic level by shouting, "We're all going to die!"

And Ben shouted back, "If you don't start pedaling harder, I'm going to be the one who kills you!"

That's when Charlie wailed, "We'll need a freaking miracle to get out of this!" Which was not a very proactive way of dealing with the situation.

I took one last look over my shoulder. The taxi was only about thirty yards away. Charlie was probably right, only a miracle would save us. But as I didn't believe in miracles, I prepared myself for certain doom.

It was probably because I was preparing for doom that I didn't immediately notice the sheep in the middle of the road, standing there like it owned the place. I only just managed to stop myself from smashing into it.

I shouted out to the others, "Watch out, there's a sheep in the road!"

Charlie hollered at me, "That's not just any sheep! That's Sheila!"

I don't know if he was right or not because another one appeared from a gap in the hedge and it looked exactly like Sheila too.

And then another.

And then a whole bunch more. There were hundreds of Sheilas, maybe thousands. Forming a bleating, baaing, woolly wall between us and the taxi.

The bald man got out of the taxi and started waving his arms around and shouting for the sheep to get out of the way, but luckily they didn't seem to understand. Probably because they were sheep. Then he said, "Oi, kids. Stop. I only want to talk to you." Which, frankly, sounded like a lie.

Ben said, "Come on, let's get out of here," and because it was a very good idea, we did. We could hear baldy shouting at us as we sped off, but there was no way any of us were stopping to talk to him.

When we felt we were far enough away, we dropped the bikes over a fence and lay down on the grass, our chests heaving and our minds racing.

I was the first to speak. "That was so close! I can't believe we got away!"

Ben said, "You're right there. I thought we were goners for sure."

Charlie sat up and, with a glazed look in his eyes and this dreamy sound to his voice, said, "It was amazing, the way Sheila and her family showed up, just in the nick of time."

Ben gave me the side-eye. "Mate, I'm not sure that really was Sheila."

"Well, I believe it was and that's enough for me. That was a real-life miracle alright."

"We were lucky, that's all," I told him. I didn't think there was such a thing as miracle sheep. But Charlie wasn't having any of it.

"No, that wasn't luck, Fred. We were saved from the Gaffer. Saved by a miracle. Sheep are very biblical animals, you know. Jesus had a whole flock of them."

"Did he?" It sounded familiar but I wasn't sure.

Ben didn't seem convinced either. "So Jesus had a whole load of sheep following him around while he was busy doing churchly things with the people of olden days? Nah, don't buy it. Wouldn't a flock of sheep have got in the way?"

"Jesus was a shepherd." Charlie said that quite proudly, like he'd just remembered.

Ben looked really confused. "I thought he did something with trees or wood?"

Charlie nodded. "He was a very talented man, was Jesus. That's why he's still so famous now. Wood, trees, shepherding, and doing churchly things with poor people . . . oh, and leopards."

"Leopards?" Now I knew *that* didn't sound right.

But because he sounded so certain when he said, "Yeah, he helped a load of leopards once and now he's helped us," I gave him the benefit of the doubt. If Charlie wanted to believe he'd experienced the miracle of Sheila the Savior Sheep, I didn't have to ruin it for him with the facts. And to be honest, the only fact I was interested in at that point was that we'd escaped the Gaffer and we were still on our way to finding Alan.

22

We find out what Beryl saw when
she got back from bingo

After our breather we decided to head off using the smaller roads to Tythegston, because the last thing we wanted was to be spotted again. If I'm honest, we were all a little jumpy, but there was no sign of the Gaffer or his taxi.

We arrived in Tythegston at 11:30 a.m., which was the perfect time for lunch. We parked our bikes by "the rec"—a patch of grass with a set of swings and a soccer goal that was leaning to one side—and walked along the main street. We had two problems to solve—hunger and our clothes (again). The cassocks didn't feel quite as petal-like in the harsh light of day, and now that the Gaffer knew what we were wearing, it was essential that we changed. Again.

We decided to stop the first person we came across

to ask where we could get something new to wear. That person turned out to be a man with tattoos up his arms and a big red beard that sparkled in the sun.

We asked him if there were any clothes shops. He laughed and said, "You won't find anything around here, but if you boys need something now, the scouts are having a secondhand sale in the village hall. You might pick up something there."

The village hall was at the end of the road. A woman wearing a velvety headband and with her collar turned up sold us secondhand scout shorts and T-shirts for three quid a bundle. It was a good deal but brought our total money down to around £31, which worried me a little. We tried to sell her the bikes to raise enough money for a train ticket, but she wasn't interested. Once we'd dropped our cassocks into a garbage bin we headed straight for the café for breakfast. I've never seen Charlie move so fast. I couldn't really blame him—my stomach felt like it was folding in on itself, I was so hungry.

The man behind the counter wiped his greasy hands down his apron, saluted us, and said, "Dib, dib, dib."

"Give us everything you've got, please, sir," Charlie said.

I elbowed him in the side and said, "Charlie, we're on a budget."

He rolled his eyes and said, "All right, *Mom.* I'll have the Big Bad Breakfast with a side of pepperoni pizza."

I ended up ordering scrambled eggs and toast. I really wanted a BLT sandwich, but I couldn't get Ben's yogurt fact out of my head. I didn't think I could ever eat bacon again knowing that pigs couldn't see the stars.

I was so hungry I didn't notice the TV set screwed into the wall next to us until I was halfway through my second piece of toast. I don't usually watch the news—it's kind of dull—but this particular news report quickly caught my attention. It caught *everyone's* attention.

Huw Jones, *South Wales Today*'s newsreader, finished telling us about the controversial new roundabout system in Carmarthen and turned to his cohost, none other than Carys Griffiths. "But traffic jams aren't a problem for the heroes of our next feature, are they, Carys?"

Carys giggled and her fluffy-cloud hair bounced around on her head. "They're certainly not, Huw. Something super has been happening in South Wales for a second time."

My mouth dropped open and the piece of toast I'd been chewing landed in my orange juice. "What now?"

The café owner came out from behind the counter, draping a dirty dish towel over his shoulder. "Have you heard about these guys? It's all over social media."

"Heard about them, we—"

I kicked Charlie under the table and shook my head.

On the TV, Carys flashed another high-wattage smile. "Yesterday, everyone was talking about the three mysterious superheroes who saved pensioner Phyllis Griffiths from a vicious attack in the village of Gileston."

"Well, Batman, Spiderman, and Supergirl have been at it again, haven't they, Carys?"

"They sure have, Huw, but this time their heroics resulted in them fending off a would-be robber."

A grainy image of me, Ben, Charlie, and the turnip-faced shopkeeper appeared on screen. I hadn't reckoned on there being CCTV footage.

Huw Jones pointed at the screen. "Now watch closely. The would-be robber walks in and Mr. David Davies— that's the shopkeeper—passes out from the sheer terror of it all. Now what happens next is interesting. The heroic trio approach the gunman. There's an exchange and the man seems to have second thoughts and leaves. He knows he's no match for South Wales's superheroes."

"What I want to know, Huw, is what the terrific threesome said to make him leave?"

"Unfortunately, Mr. Davies was not conscious during the incident, but we have him live on the phone."

Carys continued to grin at the camera. "Mr. Davies, can you tell us your impressions of the superheroes?"

A still photo of David Davies appeared on the screen. "It was like being in the presence of otherworldly beings. They weren't like you or me, they exuded power, greatness."

We were pretty awesome, but exuding power—that might have been a bit of an exaggeration.

Carys spoke again. "So you think we're dealing with the real deal, Mr. Davies? Genuine superheroes right here in South Wales?"

"I'm one hundred percent convinced."

"What makes you so sure?"

"Well, I watched them fly out of here, didn't I?"

"Fly?" Carys and I said in unison.

"Yes, I saw them fly with my very own eyes."

What. An. Absolute. Liar!

Mr. Davies was having his moment in the limelight and he was doing what he could to make it shine as brightly as possible. Even if it meant ignoring the facts.

Before Ben, Charlie, and I could discuss this unexpected turn of events, Carys and Huw threw something else at us.

"It's not just superheroes we're reporting on today though, is it, Carys?"

"No, Huw, it isn't. Our news crew have been at Three Saints Church near the village of Llampha, following a miraculous event."

I could not stop myself from shouting, "Oh, you have got to be kidding me!" That was our church. I knew, I just *knew* it was going to be *something* to do with us.

We sat there, eyes fixed on the screen, as Beryl—the caretaker of Three Saints, apparently—told a whole load of reporters about what she had witnessed early that morning. And I was right. It was *everything* to do with us.

It took Beryl a few painful moments before she realized she was on camera.

Carys said, "Beryl, could you tell us about the miraculous events at Three Saints Church?"

Beryl said, "Oh, right now?"

Carys said, "If you wouldn't mind."

"Okay then. When I got home from bingo last night, I picked up a message from Elsie. See, she'd been walking her dogs across the fields. She called to say she thought she'd heard music being played up at the old church. It was late, so I waited until morning to check it out."

"And can you tell us, Beryl, what it was that you saw?"

"I saw the most unimaginable sight. A vision, Carys. I saw a vision."

"Can you describe it for our viewers at home, Beryl?"

"I can do better than that, I filmed it on my phone."

In stunned silence, we watched the video footage of three ghostly figures floating through Three Saints's churchyard. Obviously, *we* knew it was us, on our bikes, wearing stolen cassocks. But from Beryl's vantage point, I could see why she'd thought we were a ghostly apparition. We sort of seemed to drift through the graveyard, the sun bouncing off our helmets like haloes. The early morning mist certainly added to the effect. So did Ben's *ooooooh*ing.

"That really is quite remarkable," Carys said.

Beryl's eyes were dancing. "It was them, the Three Saints. Cian, Dynod, and Elvis. I'd swear my life on it. The one at the back was definitely Dynod—the one of ample proportions."

Charlie sputtered and sprayed me with his orange juice. "Charming!"

"For viewers at home, I'll quickly explain that Three Saints used to be a place of pilgrimage. That is until the bones of the three saints disappeared."

"That's right," Beryl said.

"Can you tell us what happened next?" Huw asked.

"There's *more*?" I said.

Beryl grew more animated. She raised her fists in the air. "I knew in my bones that something miraculous was happening. And then I heard someone calling me into the church. I could hear them saying, *Beryl, Beryl—we need you, come in, Beryl. Come in, child.*"

"Yeah, whatever, Beryl," I said and shoveled in another mouthful of scrambled eggs.

I'd been feeling a little guilty that Beryl had been so completely duped . . . but this name-calling? Nothing to do with us.

"And then I saw it. The statue of the Virgin Mary was *crying*. Real tears, running down her face. It was beautiful. I stood watching her cry and I cried too. It was a *very* holy experience. We stayed there like that, crying together, for a good ten minutes."

I really thought Beryl was playing fast and loose with the facts at this point.

"What happened then, Beryl? Tell our viewers," Huw urged.

"Well, there was a huge groaning noise. Made my very bones shake. It was like the Lord was passing right through me," Beryl said, clutching her hands to her chest. I had to give it to her, she was convincing.

"And then the Virgin Mary's head exploded right off her body. Flew through the air to the other side of the church. The holy waters burst forth from the font like the River Jordan." Beryl closed her eyes for a second and then opened them again. "It was a very biblical experience."

That was one way to describe it, I supposed.

Huw spoke very softly when he said, "And what did you find then, Beryl? It was something quite amazing, wasn't it?"

"Well, the font of the Three Saints had cracked down

the middle and underneath I saw three skeletons. The missing bones of the Three Saints. Finally, they've been set free."

"Shut the fridge door!" Charlie gasped as the camera panned down the headless statue of the Virgin Mary.

There was no denying it. There were bones down there. For a moment, I thought Beryl might actually be telling the truth.

And then something in my brain clicked.

Beryl hadn't experienced a miracle. She'd experienced the aftereffects of Charlie's giant pear-and-potato deposit on century-old plumbing. The water pressure in the pipes must have blown the head off the Virgin Mary and revealed the bones of the Three Saints buried beneath.

But Beryl didn't know about Charlie's super-poo and neither did Huw or Carys. They called it a miracle on national TV. And soon everyone else was calling it a miracle too.

23

Turns out the *Barry Gazette* travels farther than we thought

We didn't pay attention to the weather report, or to the café owner babbling on at us about superheroes and saints and how it proved South Wales was God's real country. Instead, we sat there staring at each other and trying to figure out how we had ended up in the situation we were in. The blame clearly lay with Charlie's bowels.

Eventually Charlie said, "Saint Dynod. She thought I was Saint Dynod?"

"More like Saint Dyno-Rod," Ben said.

It was funny, but I gave him a look to tell him now was not the time.

Charlie pushed his plate away and muttered, "Mom's right. Ample portions make ample proportions."

Ben pushed his plate back toward him and said,

"TV adds, like, thirty pounds—you're all good, munch away."

Charlie smiled and gulped down the last of his pizza side dish.

"Do you think we should talk about what just happened?" I asked.

"Dude, where do we even begin?" Ben said.

I lowered my head onto the table. I suddenly felt really tired. "We haven't been the best at keeping a low profile. We've made the Welsh national news three times."

"And I've been in the *Barry Gazette* once," Charlie added cheerfully.

"But, Fred, don't worry. No one knows it was us," Ben said. "Everyone thinks there are real superheroes out there and that Three Saints have appeared to a woman called Beryl."

I realized my cheek was resting on a blob of congealed ketchup. I sat up and wiped my face on a napkin. "But it's all a lie."

Ben shrugged. "So?"

I glared at him. "So?"

Charlie sighed. "Yeah, what does it matter? What harm is it doing?"

I couldn't think of an answer right on the spot. "People should know the facts. We can't have people thinking miracles are real."

"Why not?" Ben asked.

"Because."

"Because?"

I wasn't going to argue any longer, especially as I didn't know the answer. So I said, "What if the Gaffer works out it's us and comes after us to wreak his revenge?"

"How's he going to do that?"

I thought about it for a moment. Ben was right. There was nothing that could lead the Gaffer to us.

Or so we thought.

Ben mopped up some baked bean juice with his last piece of bread and popped it in his mouth. "There are only two things we need to worry about now: number one, finding Alan Froggley, and number two, keeping our parents sweet. We should call them."

This made sense. Ben leaned back in his chair and called over to the café owner. "Do you have a pay phone?"

He nodded toward the corner. "Over there."

Charlie jumped up and his chair screeched across the floor. "I'll go first." Ben put a pile of coins into his hands and Charlie fed them into the phone.

"Hello, it's me, is Mom there?"

There was a long pause.

"Gabriella, it's Charlie . . . Charlie, your brother . . . Just go and get Mom." Charlie looked at us and rolled his eyes.

And then his face fell.

"What do you mean, I'm in so much trouble? Who came looking for me?"

It was obvious something was up.

Charlie frowned. "Well, what did he want? Did he give a name?"

Ben and I flashed a look at each other. I tried to hear what Charlie's sister was saying but I couldn't make out any actual words from the stream of high-pitched shrieking that was coming out of the receiver.

"But how did he know it was my sock?"

There was more loud squealing.

"Right, okay . . . okay. Okay. Can I speak to Mom now, please?"

Gabriella said something else and Charlie slumped down on a chair.

"Well, tell them I called, and it's all fine and not to worry and we'll be back this evening. Can you do that for me?"

There was more squeaking on the phone. Charlie closed his eyes.

"Gabriella . . . Gabriella . . . Gabriella!"

He banged the phone on the table three times then yelled into it, "JUST LISTEN TO ME! Everything is okay. I'm here with Ben and Fred and we'll be back soon. Make sure they all know that, okay?"

Charlie hung up the phone and looked at me, then Ben. His face had gone white. "So that didn't go brilliantly."

A very sick feeling wobbled around in my stomach. "They know, don't they?"

Charlie spoke slowly. "Gabriella said a man turned up at my house yesterday in a taxi."

"A taxi?" Ben's voice was a bit quivery.

"He asked to speak to me to interview me about my onion-eating win in Barry's annual festival. Obviously, my mom said he was mistaken, but then he showed them my photo and said he knew it was me because my name and address were on the sign-up sheet and I was named in the *Barry Gazette*."

"Right." I felt my chest get tight.

"Gabriella said Mom got hysterical as she thought I was at Fred's house, not participating in eating competitions in Wales. The man then said to Mom that he was very interested in speaking to me and gave her a sock."

"A sock? Why did he give her a sock?"

"It was my sock. He said I must have dropped it."

Charlie wasn't making any sense. "How did he know it was your sock?"

"It had a label with my name on it. Gabriella said it looked burned."

I thought about this for a moment. "He found it on his boat, didn't he—the Gaffer?"

Charlie shifted in his seat. "He must have."

Everything was unraveling.

I noticed Ben was gripping the table so hard his fingers had turned white.

"He knows who we are. He knows it was us on his boat and he knows we stole his rings." I said all that very quickly and squeakily and I could tell Charlie and Ben didn't catch any of it, so I said it again.

"What are we going to do?" Charlie asked. "Our parents are going to kill us."

"Not if the Gaffer gets to us first," Ben said.

I swallowed hard. "Should we go home?"

We sat in silence for a while, trying to process everything that had happened in the last half hour. It was a lot to take in.

Then Ben said, "We could go home and tell our parents and the police everything. But I'm also thinking in these new disguises we can make it to St. David's. If we're careful. I mean we've come this far. What's one more step?"

I blinked at Ben. "Are you absolutely sure?"

Ben smiled. "Sure."

I looked at Charlie. "What do you think?"

"My sensible side is telling me we should probably go back. But my sensible side has always been much smaller than my non-sensible side, so I say we keep going. Ben's right, we've got this far."

"I dunno," I said. "All the signs seem to be suggesting that we should go back to Andover."

And then the door to the café was flung open and a freckled boy in a scout's uniform called over to us. "The bus is leaving for the jamboree in five minutes."

Ben realized he was talking to us and said, "Where's the jamboree?"

The boy screwed up his face and said, "St. David's— duh. You coming or not?"

Ben and Charlie looked at me and Ben said, "I don't know. Fred, are we?"

And just like that we were on a bus to the final resting place of St. David.

Next stop, Alan Froggley.

24

We finally make it to the final resting place of St. David

Scouts like to sing. The whole way to St. David's, they sang. Loudly and joyfully. But even their cheery renditions of "Ging Gang Goolie" couldn't settle the weird mixture of excitement, nerves, and sheer terror I was feeling. I was convinced the Gaffer was coming after us and every time a taxi drove by I had to stop myself from hiding under my seat.

The good thing about the scouts' sing-along was that their mouths were full of "ging gangs" and not questions as to who we were and why we weren't wearing our scarf rings. They only stopped when the bus driver turned up his radio to listen to a news report about the pope's announcement that he would be coming to Wales to visit Three Saints Church.

We gave the boy scouts the slip as everyone got off at the bus station in St. David's. I couldn't believe we had finally made it. However, my sense of achievement was short-lived, because I suddenly realized that although we'd reached St. David's, I had no idea where to find Alan Froggley.

"We should go to tourist information," Charlie suggested.

This seemed like an odd idea, so I said, "Alan Froggley is hardly a tourist destination."

"Neither is Three Saints Church, but the pope is headed there on his vacation," Charlie chuckled.

"Actually, it's not a bad idea—tourist information—and what else have we got to go on?" Ben said.

I wasn't sure but because I didn't exactly have a better plan, we wandered along to the tourist information center.

Lianne—that's the lady who worked there—was very helpful and very knowledgeable. She had a kind face and reminded me of the statue of the Virgin Mary at Three Saints. Although Lianne wore a great big scrunchie in her hair and huge gold hoop earrings.

She told Charlie he could find St. David resting at St. David's Cathedral and gave us a helpful map of the local area. When we asked about Alan, she suggested that we go to city hall.

"Do they have records of everyone who lives here?" I asked.

"Oooh, maybe," she said. "But you want to talk to

Hilda. She knows most people around here. If anyone has heard of your Alan Froggley, it's her."

"Thank you, Lianne," I said.

"We will be giving you a very positive review on TripAdvisor," Ben added.

We eventually found Hilda around the back of city hall on her cigarette break. For an old lady, she wore an awful lot of makeup and had what Grams would call "quite daring" dress sense. She wore a leopard-print cardigan wrapped around her and her white-blonde hair was piled up on top of her head. She reminded me of Lady Gaga. Both the dog and the singer.

After I'd given her my dangers-of-smoking talk, I got to the real point of our visit.

"We were told you might know how to find somebody," I said, waving my hands through her cigarette smoke.

She gave a dismissive wave and all the bangles on her wrist jingled. "Who do you think I am? A private investigator?"

She didn't look like a private investigator—she had no hat or dark glasses—so I said, "No, Lianne from tourist information told us you knew everybody around here."

"Lianne—Cathy's daughter? Used to work at the bowling alley? Was dating young Eric Johnson before she broke his heart?"

Grams used to do this sort of thing—rattle on about people I didn't know and had never met.

"She had a scrunchie in her hair and big earrings?"

"Oh, *that* Lianne. Maureen's daughter. Why didn't you say so?" She puffed on her cigarette. "Yes, I know Lianne. Said I knew people, huh? Well, she's right. Who are you boys looking for?"

"Alan Froggley," I said.

She took a little step backward and steadied herself against the wall.

"Are you okay, Mrs.?" Charlie asked.

Hilda took a long drag on her cigarette and eyed me suspiciously. "Who are you to Alan Froggley?"

I didn't know what to say. I didn't want to blurt out to someone I'd just met that I was Alan Froggley's son. "My mom used to know him. I think."

"Who's your mom?"

"Her name was Molly Yates."

Hilda shook her head. "Never heard of her—" And then she stopped talking and stared at me, hard. For ages. The ash on the end of her cigarette got really long and she only flicked it when Ben said, "You know Alan Froggley or what?"

She nodded slowly. "I think you'd better come with me."

I weighed up the danger that a small elderly lady could pose to three strapping superheroes and said, "Okay, where are we going?"

"We're going to my house. I'm not talking about my Alan here."

What did she mean, *her Alan*? How could her Alan be my Alan? I wanted to ask so many questions, but from the look on her face I knew she wasn't going to answer them right then.

Hilda's car was the strangest car I'd ever seen. It had a roll-down roof, a spare tire on the hood, and she had to hit the front with a hammer to get it started. She said it was a Citroen 2CV and was made in 1965.

Charlie said, "I didn't know cars existed then."

And I was able to tell him that the first motor car was made by Karl Benz—who is the Benz in Mercedes-Benz—back in 1885. I think Hilda was impressed by my knowledge because she said, "Is that so?"

Ben said, "He has a thing about facts."

And Hilda said, "Is that so?" again.

During the drive I tried to ask her about Alan Froggley, but all she would say was, "Wait until we're home." Although she kept looking at me in her rearview mirror.

Her home was a pretty little white cottage overlooking the sea. She brought a tray of lemonade and chocolate marshmallow cookies outside and we sat on a crumbling bench and watched the waves in the sunshine.

"Where are you boys from?" Hilda asked.

"Andover," I said.

She nodded like she'd already known the answer.

"And how old are you?"

"Eleven and a bit." I really didn't want to talk about me. I knew about me. What I didn't know about was my biological father. I drained my glass. "So do you know Alan Froggley?"

She looked out at the sea. "Yes, I knew Alan. I knew him very well."

It's funny how one little word can change everything.

She said "knew." Not "know." *Knew.*

And just like that *I* knew.

"He's dead, isn't he?"

I'd said those words, but it didn't feel like they'd come out of my mouth.

"Yes, I'm afraid he is. He died almost two years ago." A little trickle of black mascara ran down her face.

I think she kept speaking after that, but I wasn't listening. I was remembering what I'd said to Ben— *people die, they die all the time*. Well, the people related to me did anyway.

A wave of sickness spread up from my toes.

It had all been a waste of time. Everything we'd done

had been for nothing. I'd got Ben and Charlie in trouble for nothing. We'd traveled across the country for nothing.

Ben and Charlie were looking at me with these worried expressions and Hilda put her wrinkled hand on my knee. I didn't want them looking at me or touching me or being kind.

I stood up and said, "I think I need to be on my own for a moment . . . if you . . . just excuse me . . ."

And then I ran. I ran out of her garden, over the hill, down toward the sea, and straight into my miracle.

25

My miracle

It wasn't anger I felt as I ran away, it was more than that. It was confusion. It was injustice. It was rage. And I needed to get it out before it got bigger than me.

When I reached the water's edge, I picked up a stone and hurled it into the sea as hard as I could. It felt good, so I threw another and another until my arms got tired and then I shouted at the sky about how unfair everything was and I screamed until my throat got sore.

Slowly, I felt a shift inside me. The rage had passed, but in its place came another feeling. A deep overwhelming sadness.

I dropped to my knees and I cried.

I cried for Grams and Mom and Alan, but also for me. Okay, a lot for me. I cried big fat sobs of sadness all for me. I cried and I cried until the tears and the snot ran dry. But I wasn't ready to stop so I forced myself to keep crying even though it wasn't really crying anymore. I was just making loud noises that sounded a lot like the seagulls that were squawking overhead.

And then someone said, "That's it, get it all out."

Embarrassment flushed through me and I swung around to see who had caught me in full meltdown mode. The sun was shining directly in my eyes, so I couldn't make out who it was.

Then they said something that made my insides jump. They said, "Come on now, my brave little soldier."

Only one person in the entire world called me their little soldier.

I shielded my eyes with my hand and blinked furiously and before I even had time to think, I heard myself say, "Grams?"

"Who else?" She stepped toward me and I could see it *was* her. "Now come here and give your old Grams a hug, I don't have long."

"But you're dead."

"Yes, I realize that, Fred. But I also realize when my grandson needs me."

"But you're dead," I said again. "You got a certificate and everything."

"A certificate? Well, that's something. But I'm not here to talk about me. I know about me. And while I might be dead, I'm still your Grams. Understand?"

I nodded even though I didn't understand. I didn't understand at all. It certainly sounded like Grams. I blinked again. It also looked like Grams—maybe a little bit more twinkly around the edges—but I would know that whiskery chin anywhere.

"Have you come from heaven?"

"Where did you think I'd be? I've washed enough of your and your father's dirty underpants to earn my place up there three times over."

"Is this real? Are you really here?"

"I'm either real or a figment of your imagination that you have produced as a way to process a recent emotional shock. I'll let you decide which. Now, do you mind telling me why we're both standing on a beach on the most western part of Wales, looking for—"

She closed her eyes for a moment and I could tell she was struggling to say the name.

Eventually she forced a smile and said, "Alan Froggley."

I made a little circle in the sand with my foot. "I thought it would all be okay, that I'd be happy if I found Alan Froggley."

Grams looked heavenward. "Lord give me strength. You thought Alan Froggley was going to make you happy? Why on earth would you think that?"

My eyes started stinging like I might cry again. "Because family makes you happy—you told me that. You even put it on one of your sweaters."

"Oh, Fred, is that what you thought?"

I noticed that while she was still sparkly around the edges, her body was starting to fade. I rubbed my nose roughly with my sleeve, then looked at her accusingly. "Well, I don't have very much family left, do I?"

"That depends on your definition of family. I think you've been using the wrong one."

"I have?"

"You have, but I'm sure you'll work it out soon enough. Now, I definitely asked for a hug quite some time ago."

She pulled me into her and filled me up with the smell of lavender and mints.

"Don't go," I said.

She held my shoulders and looked me in the eyes. Her twinkly edges were spreading across her whole body. "Don't go? I can't very well stay here, can I? And besides, you have another grandma to watch after you now."

"Another grandma?"

"Hilda. Just promise you won't go liking her more than me. Or I will come down and smite you."

"I won't," I blubbered. And then I said, "Is smiting an actual thing then?"

"You'd better believe it. Now come along, no more

tears—you'll be fine. The world's a wonderful place, Freddie. It's full of adventures and heroes and miracles, for those who go looking."

I nodded and tried to be brave and not cry.

"I love you, Fred."

"I love you, Grams."

It was getting harder to see her as the sparkles were so bright.

"Gosh, I almost forgot! Tell your father to use the picture of me in the blue cardigan on the front of my funeral program. He's picked the one of me in the peach twinset and it does nothing for my complexion."

She turned to leave.

But a thought rose up in my mind. If Grams was here, then did that mean . . . I couldn't let her go without asking. "Wait!" I shouted. "Did you see her?"

Grams smiled and nodded. "Look behind you."

I felt a hand on my shoulder. I turned.

It was my mom and she looked like stardust.

I hugged her, and she smelled of sea air and rose petals.

She rested her chin on my head and spoke into my hair. "Your dad's coming for you."

I felt the words *I love you.*

And then they were gone.

26

Where my dad finds me

It turns out that experiencing a miracle is tiring. I must have fallen asleep, because it had got cold and the tide had gone far out. I stood up and brushed the sand out of my hair. I wrapped my arms around myself and headed toward the hill I had run down from Hilda's house.

Charlie and Ben were probably getting worried. I had no idea how long I'd been away. I'd tell them I'd gone on a walk and got lost or something. I decided there and then that I wouldn't mention the chat with my dead grandmother or seeing my mom. Ben would probably think I was cracking under the stress and Charlie wouldn't be able to cope with the excitement of another miracle on top of Sheila the Savior Sheep.

As I made my way across the sand, I saw a figure unsteadily making its way toward me, waving a long stick in the air.

"Fred? Fred!"

"Dad?"

I broke into a run.

He tried to hobble a little faster on his crutches.

When I reached him I saw he looked tired around the eyes, but he'd shaved and he was even wearing a shirt instead of one of his grubby T-shirts.

"Dad, what are you doing here?"

"What am *I* doing here?" His voice quivered with anger and he pointed one of his crutches at me. "What in God's name are *you* doing here?"

Before I could reply, he'd pulled me into him. "Don't ever do that to me again, you hear? Don't you ever run away from me."

I wasn't sure if he was hugging me or strangling me. I think maybe a little of both.

He grabbed my shoulders, his crutches dangling from his wrists, and stared me in the eyes. "If you run away from me again, I'll hunt you down and I'll find you. And when I find you, you'll wish you'd run away better. You'll wish you'd run away so good that if running away was a sport you'd want to be the world champion of it. Do you understand me?"

"Not really. You're not making a whole lot of sense."

"That is because I am feeling a lot of emotions right now, Fred."

"Maybe focus on the happy emotion rather than the angry one?" I suggested.

"From now on, every second of every minute of every day, you tell me exactly what you're doing. Where you are, who you're with. I need to know *everything*. You go for a pee, I need to hear about it."

The pee thing seemed excessive, but I wasn't about to argue with a man on the edge, so I said, "Okay, Dad. I'll tell you when I pee."

"Okay. Good. Actually, maybe forget about the pee thing. But the other things . . . you need to tell me all the other things."

"Am I going to be grounded forever?"

"Longer."

I guessed that was fair enough.

His eyes softened a little. "Ben and Charlie told me about Mr. Froggley. Are you alright?"

I spotted Ben and Charlie hanging farther back on the beach with their parents. They held up their hands and I waved back.

"Yeah, Dad, I'm fine."

"They're good boys. They were worried about you racing off like that."

"I'm sorry. Didn't think."

Dad shook his head and sighed. "I'm just glad we've found you safe and well, Fred."

That was a point. How had he found me? "How did you get here from Andover so quickly?"

"Ben's dad, Becky, Charlie's mom, and me—we all headed to Wales as soon as that taxi driver showed up with that newspaper article, asking questions."

"Newspaper article?"

"The one featuring Charlie Anderson, Barry's 114th onion-eating champion."

"Oh, that one."

"Becky drove us all down last night to try and find you. We'd tracked you to Gileston and were speaking to a PC Mike when Ben called to tell us what had happened, and that you were upset."

"I'm sorry if you were worried. I thought I could get here and back without you noticing."

"Why did you come here, Fred?"

I looked toward the sea. The tide was even farther out now. "I thought there was something here I needed. Turns out I was wrong."

He put his arm around me. "You're cold. Let's get back inside and get you warmed up. And then we can start discussing how things are going to change at home. I've been a bit of a lousy dad recently . . ." He held up his hand. "Now, don't say I haven't."

I wasn't going to, but I didn't tell him that.

"I made a promise to your mom, and if your Grams was

here and could hear me now, I'd make the same promise to her. And that promise is that I will look after you and love you until the day I die."

I looked back out at the last bit of sunlight twinkling on the sea. "You know what, Dad? Maybe she is." And then I looked back at him and said, "Do you think you could put off the whole dying thing for a bit though?"

"It's a deal, if you promise to stay out of trouble."

But before I could say I'd had enough trouble for a lifetime, a taxi pulled up at one end of the beach and trouble found me again.

27

Charlie Anderson has a massive belly button and it gets us all into trouble

The Big T taxi had pulled up right where Ben and Charlie had been waiting with their parents. Dad and I started making our way toward them. The bald driver from before had a mate with him now. They got out of the front of the car and slammed the doors. Both the men were big. The driver was wearing dark glasses and had an extremely shiny bald head. The other wore a leather jacket with a Hawaiian shirt underneath. His sleeves were rolled up, I suspect to show off his muscular forearms.

Shiny-head driver guy lit a cigarette and Dad and I were close enough to hear him say, "Our Gaffer wants a word with your kids."

I stared at the smoke billowing from his mouth and thought that if there ever was a time for one of the 5,000 toxins in cigarette smoke to do their worst, this was it. Unfortunately, he remained very much alive.

"Your boss will have to go through me first," Dad said, starting toward them on his crutches.

The two men looked at each other and smirked. I wished I really was a superhero, so I could punch them both right in the face.

The Hawaiian-shirt man turned to the car and shouted, "Boss, hop-along here says you have to talk to him."

The back door of the taxi swung open.

The Gaffer stepped out. He was wearing cowboy boots.

Big Trev.

Charlie, Ben, and I looked at each other. The Gaffer was Big Trev?

Big Trev strode toward my dad. "Just so you know, I'm not after any trouble. I'm just after what's mine. You get your kids to give me back my rings and I'll leave you alone."

"We don't have your rings," Ben said.

"Well, see, I know that isn't true. I haven't been trailing your parents for nothing. Now give me my rings."

Charlie's mom stepped forward, her whole face curled into a snarl. "If our boys say they don't know anything about any rings, they don't know anything about any rings—so beat it."

Big Trev smiled. "Thing is, missus, I've got proof that

these horrible kids stole two rings from me and I'd very much like them back." He pulled open his jacket and flashed what looked like a gun at us.

"You can flash that thing at me all you like," Charlie's mom continued. "But that isn't going to turn my Charlie into a thief. We've told you they didn't take your rings."

"Actually . . ."

Everyone turned to look at Ben.

"I did have one of your rings, but we gave it to a man who was trying to rob a corner shop."

All the parents turned to Ben and shouted, "What?"

Big Trev didn't look surprised. He pulled a ring out of his pocket to show us. "I know. I've already had to buy that one back from him. What I'm after is the *other* swan ring. They're no good unless they're a pair."

"I don't get it," I said. "That ring should have been on your scarecrow. We left it there."

Dad looked at me with this expression that said, *You did what?*

"We did think you might hand it in and collect the reward money."

"It took months of planning to steal them from the *Antiques Roadshow*. Why would I hand it in after I went to all that trouble?"

"We didn't know you were the one who'd stolen them." I had to stop myself from adding a *Duh!* at the end.

Big Trev folded his arms. "Nice story, kid, but try again. I've searched the whole of Barry and there is no swan ring there. Nobody's handed it in and it certainly wasn't left on our scarecrow, which means you boys must still have it."

"We honestly don't and that's a fact," I said.

Big Trev flashed what was most certainly a scary-looking gun. "Look, people better start telling the truth or people are going to start getting hurt."

"We are telling you the truth," Ben said.

Becky put her hands on his shoulders and said, "Our Ben isn't a liar."

His dad said, "That's right, he's a good kid."

Becky said, "Yeah, he's the best."

And Ben sort of looked confused and happy and scared all at once.

"This is all very heartwarming, but you kids have already stolen my onion-eating trophy, you're not going to cheat me out of my ring."

I said, "Look, you have to believe us, we don't have your stupid ring. Do we, Charlie?"

Charlie didn't say anything. He peered out from behind his mom with one of the guiltiest expressions I had ever seen.

"Charlie!" I said.

Even his ears blushed.

"Where is it?"

He whispered to me, "I hid it in my belly button."

That kind of took me aback and I accidentally shouted, "Your belly button?"

(If you are wondering why it didn't fall out, you should take a look at Charlie's belly button. If you shout into it, I swear it echoes.)

"But why?" I asked.

"Dunno—guess for the same reason as Ben—because it was pretty,"

"What?!" Ben shouted. "That's not why I took mine. I took mine for collateral."

Charlie looked even more uncomfortable. "Yeah, that's what I meant—for collateral."

Big Trev slapped his hand on his forehead. "Enough of this nonsense." He nodded at the shiny bald guy, then nodded at Charlie and said, "Search him."

Bald guy didn't seem keen on this idea. He shifted from foot to foot and looked at Charlie uncertainly. "I don't know, boss. He's just a kid."

Big Trev wasn't taking no for an answer. "Don't argue with me. Do it. Or you'll be down at the job center faster than you can say P45."

I don't know why, it must have been the stress of the situation, but I said, "What's a P45?"

Big Trev said, "It's a certificate you're given when you quit or get fired from a job."

"You get a certificate for that?" Seemed as mad as Grams's one for dying.

"Look, stop distracting me." Big Trev turned back to baldy. "Search the fat kid already!"

Charlie's mom took a big step forward and said, "Now you listen to me. My Charlie is not fat—he is perfect in absolutely every way. You lay a finger on him and I'll snap it off."

Hawaiian-shirt man pushed Mrs. Anderson out of the way. Actually pushed her. Then he grabbed Charlie by the collar and pulled him up onto his toes. All Charlie could do was whimper.

Big Trev said, "Strip him like he stripped my scarecrows."

Charlie started flailing around, trying to break free. Mrs. Anderson got really angry and began shrieking and throwing punches at the Hawaiian-shirt man. Baldy-driver man grabbed her arm and pulled her away. Then Becky and Ben's dad grabbed ahold of baldy. He didn't like that and tried to wrestle them off. Dad plunged in, swinging his crutches around his head like he was some sort of ninja warrior. It was quite a sight.

Big Trev was not happy with how things were going. His face looked the same color as the red onion I'd eaten by mistake. He shouted, "Stop messing around and get my ring off that kid."

Hawaiian-shirt man prodded his finger on Charlie's chest and said, "Come on, fat boy—hand it over."

Well, when he said that, something inside me snapped. There was no way I was going to let another person bad-mouth Charlie. Before I knew what I was doing, I flew at the Hawaiian-shirt man and jumped onto his back, while shouting at Trev, "He's not fat—he's sturdy!"

Ben hurled himself into the fight to free Charlie too, shouting, "Or solid!" And then we ended up in this three-boy-one-man tussle on the ground. We rolled around and around on the sand, elbows and knees banging into each other. All the parents piled in too. I think Mrs. Anderson accidently hit me a couple of times and Ben definitely got hit by one of my dad's crutches. It was total carnage and it was only stopped by the sound of an ear-shattering explosion.

I pulled myself out from Hawaiian-shirt man's armpit and saw that Big Trev was pointing his gun in the air.

"Enough of this nonsense. Give me my ring before someone ends up looking like Swiss cheese."

He shot the gun skyward again.

Everyone stood still. Big Trev took a step toward Charlie.

And then my second miracle happened.

A dead seagull with a single gunshot wound fell from the sky, landed on Big Trev's head, and knocked him out cold.

It wasn't a lightning bolt, but Big Trev had definitely been smited. He'd been smited bad.

Because it's not every day you see a man knocked out by a seagull, we all—and that includes Big Trev's henchmen—stood there looking up at the sky, then down at Big Trev, who was lying with his face in the sand.

I don't know how long we would have carried on nodding like that if it wasn't for the police turning up. Two police cars screeched to a halt on the road by the beach, their sirens wailing and blue lights flashing. The third police car didn't stop but flew straight off the bank onto the sand. I could see Phyllis behind the steering wheel, a look of determination on her face. PC Mike was holding onto his helmet with his eyes closed and Albert was hanging out the back window, making a noise that sounded like a war cry. When the car came to a stop, Albert leaped out, shovel in hand, and said, "Now, which one of you lot has my family heirlooms?"

We all looked at him blankly.

"The rings!" he cried. "The swan rings! The ones stolen from the *Antiques Roadshow* because my silly sister couldn't resist showing them off." We all pointed at Big Trev, who was still lying unconscious on the sand.

When Big Trev came around, he said it felt like he'd been hit by a ton of bricks, but even the biggest seagull, the great black-backed, only weighs 4 pounds, not a ton. Now if a walrus had fallen from the sky, *that* would have felt like a ton.

PC Mike and the other police officers made quick work of arresting him and his henchmen. (We later found out that Big Trev was PC Mike's first and only arrest to date and because technically he was the one who retrieved the rings and returned them to their rightful owners, Phyllis and Albert, he got the £1000 reward money. Phyllis is making him use it to pay for driving lessons.) When we asked Mike how he knew where to find us and that we even had the rings, he told us he had super powers of his own. Charlie even believed him for a while, but Phyllis told us later that he'd picked up Big T's taxi channel on his police radio.

While all the parents talked to the police about what had happened on the beach, Ben, Charlie, and I went down to the edge of the sea to skim stones across the water.

Ben said, "I'm sorry you didn't find your dad, mate."

"It's okay. The one I've got is pretty awesome."

Charlie said, "He's not as awesome as Becky."

I was expecting Ben to have a say about that, but he didn't. Instead he said, "She's alright, I suppose."

Charlie launched another stone across the water. "Can you believe everything that's happened these past few days?"

I smiled. "I don't know, but I do know it has sure been some journey."

28

Where we say goodbye to Grams

I slid along the front pew next to Dad and turned the order of service over in my hands. There was a picture of Grams in her blue cardigan on the front—the one she had taken off at Mr. Burnley's when she was playing Monopoly. It was the picture she had asked for. I passed it to Mr. Burnley, who was at the end of our row, and he smiled.

The minister stood up and said lots of nice things about Grams. Then he did this little wrap-up of her life. It was like a sports roundup on TV when they review the goals of the season, but instead he spoke about all the best things she had done. Some of them I knew about—like her winning the marmalade competition at the Women's Institute in 2016, because I'd had to test about three thousand different recipes. Some of them I didn't—like that she had once taken three cricket wickets for Hampshire. I hadn't even known she'd played cricket. I also discovered that she'd stopped driving because she got a disease called glaucoma in her eyes, not guacamole, the Mexican food, which makes more sense.

I liked hearing new things about her, but it also made me feel sad.

I wish I'd asked her more questions.

Dad gave my shoulder a squeeze before he got up to speak. He left his crutches resting on the pew, took a piece of paper from his pocket, and placed it on the lectern. Just looking at him standing up there on his own made me want to cry. My chin started to do that wobbling thing it does just before the tears come. I thought I was probably going to dissolve into floods, but then Hilda stopped scratching her nicotine patch and put her hand on top of mine and I felt a little better.

She's not your regular kind of grandma, Hilda, but she's doing okay, by the way. I won't say "brilliant" because Grams might hear, and I wouldn't want to get smited. I still think she might have had a hand in the seagull incident.

Dad cleared his throat, straightened his tie, and took a deep breath. "I'm a very lucky man to have known Iris. It's thanks to her that I have experienced love and happiness in my life, through her daughter, my Molly, and through her grandson, my son Fred.

"Iris taught me what it means to be a family. When

my Molly died, I didn't know what to do. Some of you will remember I was in a pretty bad way. But Iris opened her heart to me and took me in. She taught me how to be a father. She showed me that it is not the blood that flows through our veins but the love in our hearts that brings us together."

His eyes went all watery and he looked at me. "One thing I've learned is that even though people are no longer with us, it does not mean we have to stop loving them."

Hilda gave my hand another squeeze and her bangles jingled.

I closed my eyes for the next part because I didn't want to look at Grams's coffin as it was carried out. I told myself she wasn't really inside. She was somewhere else. Somewhere where she had twinkly edges.

When I opened my eyes again, I was surprised to see Ben and Charlie standing at the front of the church. They both gave me these small smiles, then turned and nodded to the minister.

The first few bars of a song started playing over the speaker system. (The church in Andover is a little more modern than Three Saints in Wales.)

I recognized the tune immediately.

Ben and Charlie started the singing.

"One more step along the world I go . . ."

Soon everyone in the congregation was joining in.

Dad leaned in and whispered to me, "Your friends suggested you might want this played. When I listened to the lyrics—about traveling on this journey through life together—it seemed perfect."

"It is," I whispered back.

And then I heard Charlie and Ben ribbiting.

Dad stared at them and then at me with this baffled look on his face. I couldn't help but laugh. And that's when I realized what Grams had been talking about. My definition of family *had* been wrong. It's a bit like pigs not knowing about the stars. I needed to change my viewpoint to see what had been there all along.

29

The fact about miracles

When I got into bed the night after Grams's funeral there was something hard beneath my pillow. I stuck my hand under and pulled out my *Things I've Done Which Would Make Mom Proud* book. I didn't remember leaving it there. I flicked through the pages and found that every single line had been filled in. There wasn't a single blank space left. Even the margins were crammed with Dad's scribbled writing.

Everything I'd ever done was in there. My first words, my first steps, the first time I tied my shoes. When I didn't hit Barry Williams at school even though he called me an idiot. When I *did* hit Barry Williams for calling me an idiot a second time. When I gave my ice cream to a little girl who'd dropped hers . . . And so on. He'd remembered it all. When I got to the back page, I saw he had written, *To my son, my miracle.*

Miracles.

At the beginning I told you I wasn't sure miracles really happen. According to Wikipedia, *a miracle is an extraordinary and welcome event that is not explained by natural or scientific laws.*

When you look at that definition, it's easy to rule out a lot of miracles.

Beryl the church warden was wrong about her vision in the churchyard that morning.

David Davies didn't see three superheroes fly out of his shop.

And PC Mike didn't witness superhero strength the morning we pinned Albert to the pavement.

But like Grams said, maybe I'm using the wrong definition. Maybe I need to change my viewpoint.

Because while it wasn't the Three Saints who caught the nation's imagination, it was *us* Beryl saw being set free. And while we didn't fly, Mr. Davies did see three best friends taking off on an adventure. And maybe PC Mike saw a different kind of strength when we rugby-tackled Albert. Because, from what I've learned, superheroes don't wear capes and they don't need bulging biceps. Superheroes are the people who show up for you when you need them. A bit like family.

And maybe I didn't see my Grams or feel my mom's love down by the sea on the most western part of Wales. Maybe I made it all up. Maybe I was dreaming.

I can't know for sure.
I can't say it's a fact.
But maybe, just maybe, I did.
And for me, that's enough.

THE END

Acknowledgments

Firstly, I'd like to thank THE best agent out there, the super miraculous Sam Copeland who kick-started my journey into publication. And what a journey that has been. Thank you—for everything. I've had the best time.

Simon Boughton, my wonderful US editor at Norton Young Readers, thank you for taking on Freddie. And for working through all the many Briticisms I included. There were a lot.

Rebecca Hill, my editor, and Becky Walker at Usborne UK, two shining gems of the publishing world. Thank you for your vision and your enthusiasm for Freddie. Working with you both has been an absolute dream and I feel so lucky!

To my sister, Caroline Bowne, one of the funniest people I know. You are a wonderful human being for reading all of my rough scribblings. And to Josie Shah, Katie Murray, and Polly Scobie for going through the pain of reading my scratchy first drafts too.

Acknowledgments

Thanks also to the amazing Catherine Johnson at Curtis Brown Creative and my writing group pals I found on that course—you know who you are. My SCBWI writing group for all your helpful comments and support. To Stuart White at Write Mentor and Carolyn Ward—the best cheerleader a girl can have. And my American author pal, Josh Levy, for being a great sounding board.

To the children at St Margaret's, Durham—Year 6 Silver and Gold classes (2018–19) and Year 3 Orange and Purple classes (2019–20) in particular—thank you for being total little rock stars and a joy to teach (mostly).

And finally, to all the extraordinary, hilarious, and talented kids I've had the privilege to teach over the years: You are all your own miracles, and I thank you for the endless inspiration you have unwittingly provided. (I wasn't joking when I said if you misbehaved, I'd put you in a book.)

If I've missed anyone out, please forgive me, you know what I'm like. I'll buy you a drink to make it up to you.